Jennifer Phillips

The Red Woman and Water Lilies

AmErica House
Baltimore

First printing

ISBN: 1-58851-651-2
PUBLISHED BY AMERICA HOUSE BOOK PUBLISHERS
www.publishamerica.com
Baltimore

Printed in the United States of America

Dedicated to Grandma, for your love and faith, and to Robin, for being who you are

Chapter 1

The heat poured over her skin like a blanket. Its thick taste left beads of sweat across her entire body. Divina barely noticed as she walked the dirt road leading her further and further back into the New Orleans' swamp land. She lived this place. Its imprint was racing through her blood, and her heart beat that blood with a strength few individuals possessed. The trees had capes of torrid air. The heat tied everything to the ground, and there was no running away from it.

One sharp turn and the thickness of the brush vanished. What was left was an open space and the house: The house in all its divine enchantment. Divina was born here a mere twenty years ago. Her brothers were born here too. This estate, as they called it, was nothing more than a beaten and broken frame filled with ghosts from the past. It was white once, at least that is what Divina believed, because she had never actually seen it white. That didn't matter to her. She could see it if she squinted her eyes just so. Then, there it was, the large porcelain fountain spitting out clear water high into the arms of the golden angel who waited there to catch it in all her statue's glory. The grass was green and lush, and the breeze whipped all the vines around the house showing their bearings of red fruit and bronze leaves. The great stairs were magnificent and held no debris from rain nor storm. It beckoned royalty to walk upon it. The white paint shined and the windows were so clean that you could see the people inside the house.

Divina saw shadows and made herself believe that they were people. She made them into who she needed them to be, people she had never known but heard so many stories about. People she loved, and people she created. As Divina looked on, a flash of lightning crashed above her. She quickened her steps, and the mirage she had just envisioned vanished. The broken fountain loomed a dark shadow; the yellow and brown vegetation surrounded all her view. The house recovered its pale old ivory coloring, and the windows were black as night. She reached the stairs of the house, and she jumped from side to side in order to place her feet in the few clear spaces until she reached the front door.

The crying of a six-year-old boy echoed off the walls. Divina kicked off her boots without soles and took long strides until she reached the kitchen. That is where she found the source of the crying. Belinda, Divina's elderly aunt, was there standing above the frightened child and holding a small clear bottle. Claude was Divina's youngest brother. He took medication for a heart disorder. It was inherited from their parents. Although Claude was the only one of the three children to show symptoms, the other two were always on the watch for them. Belinda was trying desperately to coax Claude to take his medication. It was always an ongoing battle.

"Now, young man, you *will* take this!" Belinda's tone defied all who would dare argue against her.

She was an old woman, about sixty-four, but no one really knew for sure. She wore elaborate jewelry. In fact, Divina had only seen her without jewelry once. That was when Rebecca died. Rebecca was Belinda's sister and the children's mother. In the rush and shock of the middle of the night, Belinda had flown down the stairs with a long robe, and her hair tied back, but absent was all her jewelry. That was the only time. Otherwise, she had a ruby bracelet with thick gold accents, five large necklaces, four diamond rings, a sapphire ring, and large opal earrings. These elegant accessories were offset by her wardrobe. Belinda always wore a bathrobe as if she was constantly ready to go to sleep. They had flowers or paisley prints or deep richly colored stripes. And she always wore bedroom slippers. She had fourteen pairs to go with all her robes. Divina knew as she watched the anguished aunt trying to help Claude that Belinda really didn't have much authority around this place.

"No! No!" The little boy screamed until he noticed Divina's entrance.

"Thank God," Belinda muttered out loud to no one in particular.

Divina took the bottle, grabbed Claude in one swoop of her left arm, and propped him up on the big wooden table. He kicked his feet against air but had stopped screaming. She looked at her brother. "Take it, please, Claude."

He knew there was no other way out now. He took the medicine, and then he milked it for all it was worth by making faces and noises and, for a finale, rolling around on the floor. Belinda and Divina watched him in silence, exchanging bored glances with each other until he had finished.

"Where's the other," asked Divina, as she moved her head about, searching for her other brother. She wasn't surprised. He was young and adventurous and always running off searching for himself.

"Edgar is probably out looking for birds with a sling shot," Belinda said as she sat in a chair at the table. She was exasperated with Edgar always. He was quick and didn't like authority.

"He is the same as I was, Belinda, when I fourteen," Divina said, laughing softly.

Claude had crawled up into her lap, and Divina stroked his silky brown hair. It fell almost over his light blue eyes. He tried so hard to see everything because he needed to know what and where everything was at all times.

"Can I go find Mary," Claude asked, batting his eyes in an attempt to look cute.

"May you?" Divina waited for him to make the correction.

"Fine." He muttered while glaring at his big sister. "May I go find Mary?"

The loud creaking of Mary's wheelchair could be faintly heard down the hall. Divina looked toward the sound, smiled, and shook her head yes. Claude jumped off Divina's lap and ran out of the room.

When Rebecca, Divina's mother, had lived in this house, Mary was the maid. Mary cooked and cleaned and did the laundry. Back then she was old. Now, she wheeled herself about in a rickety old wheelchair. Most of her hair was gone, but the few strips of gray that were left were brushed daily. Then, Divina would pull them back for Mary in order to help hide at least some of the missing hair. Mary dressed well, usually in nice pants and a white tank top. It didn't vary much. She had never worn a uniform, and even if she had, it would have been retired long ago. Divina loved her as much as family and therefore could never let her go. Mary knew she was forever safe and welcome in this house with these people.

Divina stood up from the table as Mary wheeled herself in with Claude at her heels. A chair was moved so that Mary could move to the table. Belinda and Mary were good companions although in Mary's old age she was beginning to weaken. She forgot things, and it was hard to remember a time when she could carry the weight of a full conversation. Belinda was patient, though, and loved Mary like a sister. When Mary's mind was good, as it was on certain days, she was keen and full of questions. Today was one of those days.

Divina stood at the sink in the kitchen, one of the few that still worked. She ran some water and put it on the oven to boil. Divina's long hair was tied back with a piece of cloth, and a smudge of dirt was etched across her cheek. Her blue eyes were wide and awake. Unlike most days, she wore a pastel flowered dress that came to her ankles. It was Rebecca's dress, and Divina loved to wear her clothes as much as possible when she was to be seen. Usually, she wore work clothes and looked like a dirty child. Today, she looked like the woman she was.

Mary looked at Divina and asked, "So, did you see John today?" Divina turned to her and gave her a look of definite annoyance. She smiled eventually, though, and that lit up her entire face. "I'll take that as a yes. How is his farm? Have you a ring on your finger yet?" Mary craned her neck to try to see Divina's hand.

"His farm is fine, Mary. I said no to him again. I will say no to him next time, too, and the time after that. It is too soon to tell such things."

"Divina!" Mary's voice made Divina jump a little. It was harsh and overbearing and tried to hold authority that it did not own in Divina's eyes.

"Yes, Mary?" Divina felt that she had the patience of a saint at times like these.

"How long have you known John? Since you were born. He is a good man, is he not?"

"He is, Mary, but--"

"But nothing," replied Mary.

Divina retrieved some noodles from a cupboard and put them in the water. Then, she stirred with ferocity.

"Mary," Belinda said softly, "look. Here comes Edgar." Divina smiled at Belinda. Her attempt at diversion was successful as Mary now focused her full attention on the approaching boy.

Edgar was tall now, almost as tall as Divina. She wasn't sure what to do with him. Living in a house with two ladies for eight years can do that to a person. He liked dirt and sweat and no emotions. He liked to pretend he was invincible, and he was looking for things to challenge his good sense. Divina caught him diving off shallow rocks or getting too close to danger at least once a week. She was a savior to him. Edgar only trusted her. He didn't want to be taught who he should be or given rules to live by. Edgar looked exactly like his father, and at times, acted like him. Sometimes it hurt Divina to look at him. He didn't really remember. Not the way that she did.

When night takes over the house, terror can set in easily. It can bring back voices and footsteps and sounds. Divina knew this all too well. In the beginning, Edgar would have these terrible dreams. His screams would cover the imaginary ones. So, Divina began to sing at night. She didn't know many songs, and she wasn't very good, but Mary had an old church book. Until everyone was asleep, Divina would sing as she went about the house. She would clean or close windows or peek in the rooms. Some nights she would just walk and walk. It soothed her soul because she knew what lingered ahead. It would be silent in the house, and she would be the only one not calmed into sleep. Edgar slept through the night again. Claude grew up listening to it. As the years passed, Mary and Belinda said she was a regular professional singer, but Divina just laughed because she knew they hadn't heard any singing for so long that their table of reference was probably more off than they realized. They felt the peace that wrapped itself around the words that she sang. The faith that was renewed in praising God after what He had taken from them.

Edgar moved in rhythmic, animal-like proportions. He could creep out of the house at any time and be undetectable. He trained himself to be like that which he wished he were. He trained himself to feel freedom and to feel the breeze as his air. He followed the earth's example as she breathed in and out. He thought he took air into his lungs with the world. Who was anyone to challenge that? As the sun set on that night it reminded them of the nights of long ago. Edgar smiled gently to see everyone gathered together. Then, without a word, he walked with a man's gait towards his room at the other end of the house. The three women in the kitchen watched him. His smile was reminiscent of Mr. Hamilton's face. Mr. Hamilton was Rebecca's husband and the children's father. At least, Divina and Edgar's father to be sure.

* * * * *

Mr. Hamilton was known as a kind man. He was tall and strong and had a deep voice. He was very recognizable. If you saw him once, then you would remember him the next time you saw him. His hair was almost black at times, and his eyes were almond brown unless he was angry. On the occasions that his anger infiltrated him, then his eyes would grow black like his hair. He was clean cut, and his chin had a chiseled outline that made him attractive. He was a businessman's son, and when he decided he wanted a life as a farmer, he was looked down upon. Mr. Hamilton's father did not hear that his son wanted to live his life as a farmer. What he did hear was that his son wanted to live his life as a poor farmer. Mr. Hamilton was an educated man, an intelligent and, some would even say, brilliant man. Everyone said that he would do just fine, even as a farmer. So, his father agreed to let him try out his little idea. Mr. Hamilton borrowed some money from his father and bought the biggest lot of land in the middle of where developers said the industry would boom in the future.

In other words, no one was there yet, and Mr. Hamilton had just made a life in seclusion, away from civilization in New Orleans, Louisiana. Although it wasn't well known, this land had been in his family before, generations ago. Mr. Hamilton had roots in this place that were deeper than just the ground. He had studied all about his craft, so he knew as much as you possibly could about farming without ever actually being involved with it. He learned fast.

Meanwhile, Rebecca Whitfield had moved herself across the world again. She flew in from her home country of France to America. There, she studied architecture in a prestigious New York university. She had an eye. Not only was Ms. Whitfield rich, but she was goddess beautiful. Her long mane of hair was the color of the sun, and she had the features of great beauties everywhere. Her voice was just the right tone, and she carried herself not to be seen as beautiful but just to be seen. People stopped to look at her. While off with one of her high-class friends, she found out about the New Orleans's riverboats. Her friend told her what a fabulous time it was and mentioned that she should come along next time. Rebecca went to New Orleans in order to have some nice champagne and gamble and look at how life was down south. She didn't know then that she would never leave New Orleans for good.

Mr. Hamilton had big plans for his farm. He was rarely distracted from his big plans, but his father often called him to ask him for favors. They were always public favors, such as the one where Mr. Hamilton was to escort his father on the riverboats during one of the big celebrations. There would be lots of media there, and it would look good for the Hamilton family to be present. He dressed in his best black suit, slicked his hair back, and joined his father for their public image. Every man in their presence wanted to be them, and every woman wanted to be with them.

The biggest and most extravagant riverboat, The Prowess of the Mississippi, was the Hamiltons' final destination. Rebecca had been on the boat for about half an hour.

She had arrived in town only that morning. She didn't really seem bored, but she couldn't figure out what all the fuss was over either. She walked around the riverboat until she found herself outside, looking down into the water. She placed her arms on the banister, and she watched the sky. A fist of laughter swung at her from inside the boat. She turned her head, and through an open door, there he was. She stared.

Mr. Hamilton was toasting a mutual acquaintance of both his father and himself. He rose his glass high and peered around the room. It was full of the same people he had grown up with, the same girls he had seen in college, and the same coworkers of his father. He was glad to be out of it and to be away from it all. His laugh rang loud and true, and the wind carried it about the boat. Everyone smiled in recognition of the man who they had seen as a boy not long ago. His gaze drifted out of the boat, and he saw this woman staring at him. She stood alone, her long gauze dress blowing behind her in effortless mercy with her hair's movement. He handed his champagne glass to the closest person to him and walked outside. She drew him in like prey, and he didn't even care.

"Do I know you?" His eyes searched her, and she felt a chill. He didn't look at her; he looked through her.

"I'm going to marry you," she said simply.

He took his suit jacket off and wrapped her in it. Then, he placed his arms over the banister. They watched the water spinning beneath them and the sky above them in the purity of silence. By the next morning, they were married.

Mrs. Rebecca Hamilton was introduced to the public that very afternoon. Mr. Hamilton's father had steam practically coming out from his ears when he heard the news. "Why on earth would you do this so soon," he asked his son.

"Sometimes," Mr. Hamilton said as he looked over at Rebecca, "you have to go with your gut in order to make life worth living."

His father shook his head as he watched the couple walk away. He knew intuitively that this woman was pure fire, and his son was pure gasoline. He returned to his life and waited for the eruption.

The ride was long to Mr. Hamilton's house. Rebecca impatiently waited to see what awaited her in this rich man's manor. She hadn't quite realized that he was a farmer, but when she saw the place she knew for sure. She set her foot down on that ground, and he watched her. His big almond eyes watched, and the speck of white in his pupils had a tense, biting fear that she would scream she couldn't live like this. He looked to the sky, which had forewarned of storm all day. The thunder exploded and hurt her ears. Then, the downpour began. He had no idea that he would be this vulnerable. He wanted to cover her from this place, to protect her delicate hair from the thrashing wind. He thought himself a fool. What kind of man makes a bride of this woman and brings her here? He knew his mansion was for her, but this place? This life? Her light French accent would be foreign to all the wanderers that traveled these parts. They would frighten her.

She stood there, her hair matted and her white dress thoroughly wet. He could see through it, all the way through her. Her ribs went in and out. Her breathing was inhibited, and she parted her lips slightly, her back to him as she stood twenty feet away from where he stood. She looked up at the darkness that surrounded her.

"I'm sorry!" He yelled over the storm, and he didn't look at her. He looked at his hands, these hands that built this place, which built this loneliness that he hadn't known existed until he had Rebecca standing there.

In a slow bird motion, her arms came from her sides, and she lifted them to be horizontal with her shoulders. Then, she began to spin. And she flew; she spread her arm-like wings and flew over the land. She cradled it in her soft finger gestures, and she spun.

Mr. Hamilton's eyes moved to her, the way her hips swayed with the rain. She faced him, and he searched her again, and she smiled. Her arms were in the air, and the noise of the storm on the land and in the woods covered everything.

"I am home," she yelled to him

"What?" He yelled back, cupping his right ear with his right hand. He couldn't hear anything over this storm.

Instantly, she walked so fast that it seemed she took two steps, and she was there.

No pausing, no warning. She grabbed his neck and kissed him. It took him a second, but he figured it out and grabbed her waist. He picked her up and swung her about as her lips never left his. So, it began.

* * * * *

12

Days passed as they often did in Divina's life. She hadn't recognized the moment when she had stopped being the child she was not long ago. Sometimes she thought that she had grown up with the snap of fingers, and other times, she felt as though she had never grown up at all. She was restless in this life, working this broken land, breathing this air that filled her every pore.

Mornings were bittersweet and left a salty aroma over the ground that the children walked. Claude slept until the day was half gone while Edgar, well, no one really acknowledged what time Edgar began his days. Divina listened for him each morning.

She was always the first one up. Edgar would move like a cat until he was out of the house, until he was free from even the mere sight of it. Divina wondered what he did and who, if anyone, he was with. Part of her worried and part of her hoped. She had bigger plans for Edgar. Edgar had bigger plans for himself.

If there had been a rooster on this farm, then it surely would not have been awake at this hour. The sun was nowhere to be seen; she hid her face below the horizon. Edgar knew where she was, his loyal sun. He could tell that she waited for him just below the trees. She was taunting him. She was invisible, but Edgar could feel her just below the surface. He knew it wouldn't be long before she would rise. He stretched his legs, which were too long. His feet hung over the edge of his bed. That was all right; he slept curled up like a kitten anyway. He pulled on old jeans and a tee shirt over his long johns. To the average listener, there was only silence. To Edgar, the booming noise was intrusive and bothersome. He couldn't sleep through it anymore than a person could sleep through an earthquake. The bugs outside were buzzing, speaking their piece before the dawn. The trees were crashing. Branches struck with the force of the wind. Grass howled. The earth was awake.

Small, scratchy sounds were quick and calculated. Divina knew instantly. Her instinct told her that he was gone now. She arose from her bed, leaving the warm indentation crying for her return. She looked back longingly, only for a second. Then, she swiftly went to the window and pulled back a ratty curtain to watch the creature disappear into the woods. He was a crusader going through thick brush, and he left no trail behind. It was as if he had never been there.

Today was different than most days. It was Wednesday. Today was the one day of the week when Divina at least had an idea what Edgar would be doing. He would work for John today. He would get paid too much for too little work and bring it home to the family. Divina did laundry while she waited for his return. She thought of John, of his proposal. She wrung the laundry tighter and tighter until Belinda screamed at her to calm down and pay attention.

"Where is your mind, child?" Belinda's eyes were full and wide. She looked ready to get out a wooden spoon and hit Divina's wrist like she was a two-year-old.

"Sorry," Divina muttered, wiping her brow. It was early morning and already too humid for words. She didn't want to think of John.

John Cordston was a man of work and family. He was raised on his land. Divina could relate to him. She had played with him as a child, and she had danced her only dance with him as a teenager. John wasn't the man that she wanted, but he tried to be the man that she needed. He wanted to take care of her, to take her away from what made her twenty-year-old eyes look so old and weary. He was a good man, as Divina was often told. She thought of a life with him. She imagined how good it would be to get everyone out of that house. She could make whatever life she wished for them. John would send Edgar off to school, and Claude could play with children his own age. Belinda could find a tea group and sew quilts and find joy in things that were no longer joyful for her. Mary could get a good doctor to look at her. She would be well taken care of and wouldn't want for anything.

Divina sat down and put her head on her crossed arms. She sighed. She thought of the life that she would live. She would automatically have to start having children, as John often told her that time was wasting away. Inside her head she screamed, "I am only twenty years old!" She would have to wait on him hand and foot. Divina often told him that he wanted a maid and not a wife.

"But I could never love a maid the way that I love you," he said to her.

"Maybe you should go out and find one, and perhaps she might surprise you," Divina would shoot back.

It was not that Divina did not love John. She loved him a great deal, but she wasn't in love with him. She didn't feel fire when she looked in his eyes; she felt frustration and resentment. John didn't think women needed opinions because there were men for that. It was a terribly old and unintelligent miscalculation. The fact that he mentioned it so often would be

14

the unintelligent factor. Of course, he fell in love with the one woman who had more opinions than most of the men he knew.

John would wait for her, and she knew it. He would wait as long as it took. He never dated; he never socialized. He just loved her. It was an honest love, a great love.

He paid Edgar so that she would have enough food on the table. He gave her a confidant, a friend. He knew all there was to know. He had been there through it all. He watched her climb trees and swim in muck swamps when she was eight. He held her hand when she first broke her leg, and he drove her to the hospital for every injury. She was jumping rocks that were too high and climbing down vines that were too weak. She had to know what she was capable of, and she learned. He gave her the only Valentine's Day card he had ever made. She still had it. It was the only one she ever remembered. When she was fifteen, she gave him his first kiss. Granted, it was only on the cheek and was a thank you for finding Edgar when he was lost, but he thought of it all the same. John picked out the suits for the boys to wear at the funeral for their parents. He took care of her family as much as she would let him.

Why, then, wouldn't Divina marry such a man? It would be a good marriage, she knew. He wouldn't leave her or intentionally hurt her. He would do his best, and how can anyone ask for more than that? She was okay, though. She took care of everyone. She had Edgar in school, except for the summers such as this one. She took care of the house, she tended as best she could to the farm. She knew it wasn't her fault that the place was broken down. Everyone was healthy, and she made things all right. She didn't need to marry John. She wasn't even sure if she wanted to get married. It didn't really have anything to do with John. She wanted to see the world, and she wanted to look, with her own eyes, upon those things that she had only seen in books. The colors, she had decided, would be so much more vivid. Her heart would be filled with overwhelming happiness at such a moment. She wanted her life to have moments such as those. She knew if she married John, she would never leave this place. Although she loved it, she didn't love it enough to stay with John. If she stayed, it would be because she could somehow fix the farm. It would somehow be as it once was in all its splendid glory.

The farm was once an amazing feat. It had ripe and luscious crops. It had birds enveloping the background with their smooth harmonies. It reeked of life and prosperity.

Divina was only a child when it crumbled. She had glimpses of memories, but nothing concrete. There were only a few darkened pictures left behind to show what the place once was.

Chapter 2

Mr. Hamilton and Rebecca were elite socialites. Within the first month of their marriage, they were throwing extravagant parties. To outsiders who came in, they looked so in love. In reality, Mr. Hamilton knew that Rebecca would not be happy living like this for very long. He tried to hold onto it for as long as he could.

The first year, the crops were modest. Mr. Hamilton was not pleased with average. He strove harder with Rebecca at his side. Rebecca, who wanted to be the talk of the state, of the world, was always pushing subtly for an explosion onto the scene. By the second year, the Hamiltons had done more than explode. They were volcanic. Mr. Hamilton worked the land while Rebecca let the maids wait on her. She took some professional voice lessons. She drew out more architectural plans. They were very good, and famous and prestigious people were impressed with them. These people did not understand why such talent lived in the back woods of Louisiana. She found offers and such that came her way, but it was obvious that her location inhibited her. It wasn't that she had a serene passion for the work, but it kept her busy, and most importantly, it kept her well known.

Mr. Hamilton had an amazing second year. His crops were sought after for their quality. He had buckets of money, and they were on top of the game. It was exciting and exhilarating. Everyone knew who they were when they ventured into the towns nearby.

Rebecca wanted to travel. She wanted to show her loving husband her home in France. She wanted to take cruises and eat local cuisine. She wanted to shop in Paris and see the opera in Sydney. She was ready to flaunt her wealth. Mr. Hamilton appeased her, at first. Of course, he couldn't drop everything and go away. Rebecca didn't understand. He wanted the third year to be better than the second year. He told Rebecca that he had to work to do that, and that he couldn't just jaunt off with her whenever he pleased. The whirlwind settled down. Each day became a ritual.

"I'm going mad!" Rebecca would exclaim when Mr. Hamilton would be too busy for her or for anything that didn't deal with the farm. He tried, though. He made her elegant, romantic meals. He took her for late night walks under the stars. He would kiss her with such passion that she felt a tornado was swirling inside her belly. There were moments when she knew what it was like to actually be in love for a lifetime.

Rebecca flew back to France not long after the whirlwind slowed down. She went to see old friends and tell them how well she was doing. She wore expensive clothing and elegant jewels. Her family welcomed her with open arms and was amazed at how well she looked for being out in the country for so long. They didn't understand how she could live like that day after day, moment after moment. Rebecca tried to tell everyone stories, but once she finished a small anecdote from a big get together or a detailed description of some of her new friends' wardrobes, she drifted back into the isolation and humility that came along with her new life.

While sipping some preposterously expensive drink on a tier, Rebecca sat overlooking a majestic scene with her friend, Blanche. The two had gone to the same prestigious school together. Blanche was the friend that Rebecca had known and trusted the longest out of every person she knew. As Rebecca looked out over the scene before them, Blanche stared at her friend who was suddenly such a strange and foreign creature.

"What are you thinking about, my dear," asked Blanche. Her eyes covered Rebecca's face. It was masked in softly dim light and as beautiful as it had always been, but there was something remarkably altered about her friend.

"I was thinking of home, I must admit," Rebecca announced with a small smile and a quick beverage sip. She felt the breeze around her, and although she had arrived not long ago in France, she yearned to leave. It was not as exciting as it had once been. The glamour was still there, but her heart wasn't it in anymore.

"Tell me one thing, and I promise I will let it go," Blanche quietly said.

"Go ahead. I won't take offense at anything you have to say. I know you, Blanche, you mean well. So, shoot," Rebecca remarked. She waited gingerly and wondered what her friend would ask. What exactly would this one question be that could explain everything?

"Do you love him, Rebecca," asked Blanche as she sat down her cup on a nearby table.

Rebecca brought a drink to her lips and peered at Blanche over the top of the glass with her glowing eyes. She looked at the sky, and she traced the glass with her fingers. Blanche waited and watched Rebecca try to summon the correct words to answer her question. "Yes. I do love him," answered Rebecca.

Blanch leaned forward and put her hand on top of Rebecca's. "Good then. There is nothing more to explain, is there?"

"I love him…" Rebecca said once more, and then she looked at Blanche with a far away glance and a sad look in her face, "in my own way."

Blanche sat back in her chair and shrugged her shoulders. She knew her friend too well to say anything more. Blanche knew that for Rebecca to admit such a thing was not only irrational but also unthinkable. The fact that she used the word love gave Blanche some hope, but she also knew that her dear friend knew herself too well for her own good. Rebecca could never be fully happy for long. She had to be rearranging or changing things in her life to fit the times of her moods and her heart. Rebecca had a big heart when it came to certain things, and it just happened that men and relationships were not one of those certain things.

Rebecca returned to her nameless land. Mr. Hamilton went about his daily business, and all faded and spun to dust. A simple morning came, but it was unlike any other. Mr. Hamilton awoke, but Rebecca was gone. A shadow in his soul covered him; its cold and brisk breath turning him inside out. He knew she would leave someday, but surely, he thought, today was not someday.

She sat on the great steps of the mansion. All she wore was one of his dirty work shirts. Her hair wasn't combed; her face wasn't washed. There was an accumulation of dirt claiming the pink flesh under her fingernails. He saw her and relief washed over him. She didn't even turn around when she spoke. "Things will never be the same," she said.

Mr. Hamilton was unsure whether she was talking to herself or whether she knew he was there. He calmly, and in a fit of grace, placed himself next to her. He had never seen her as she was at that moment. There was an earth about her now.

She extended her arms before her. The harsh fabric of the shirt swallowed her in silent protest. Her body was used to the finest materials. Her skin was used to soft water and fragrant oils. Her fingers were in shock from the foreign calluses that visited her daily. There was something new in her face, a raspberry glow.

"Are you all right," he asked her with simple urgency. Her skeleton wanted to be visible through her skin. She was too alive to be so ghost-like. "I'm pregnant." Flat and drafty, her voice sat on the stairs between them.

His chin dropped slightly. She kicked at some loose dust near her china feet. Big and stunned, a hearty laugh swarmed over them. He rejoiced as her ethereal expression settled into her face's youth. Divina was on her way.

* * * * *

The sky was littered with purple. The blue undertones were thrashing and bursting. Punching all that stood in the way, the smoldering heat refused to let even a breath of breeze enter the shade. Edgar would be back soon, and John would be with him. The two old ladies were primping in their quarters. Claude was incessantly bored. Divina threw together some vegetables for a stew. In yet another dress, this one with tiny blue flowers, she swooped around the kitchen with a bowl of yellow batter cradled in her arms. A loose and slightly crooked braid dressed her head. She hummed softly, and Claude was sprawled out in the corner of the kitchen.

Edgar bounded through the doorway. His skin was darkened by dirt and tan. She looked clean and polished. His face registered no emotion as he walked over to her in defined steps. He then proceeded to look closely at the batter she was pouring into a square pan.

"Back away," she commanded as she shook the spoon and empty bowl at him.

He grabbed at the bowl, and she squealed in girlie horror. Claude watched in splendor at the play in front of him. Divina quickly lost the battle as Edgar swiped the bowl from her. With one foul finger, he reached down and retrieved what was left of the batter. He licked his soiled finger slowly and with such purpose.

Divina glared at him while trying not to look amused. "Go wash up," she told him. He plopped the bowl down on a far away counter after cleaning it with his workman fingers. She couldn't help but notice his thin arms covered in vein muscle. He was his father's son.

"John will be along soon," yelled the coarse voice in the other room. Edgar sounded deep and rough, and it was almost unfamiliar to the family. He barely spoke anymore.

Claude scowled. Divina turned away in secret light. She knew it was wrong to let Claude know that she appreciated his distrust of John.

Mary and Belinda entered the kitchen and crooned in the last of the day's light. They waited impatiently for John to appear. He came over every second Wednesday of the month, and every second Wednesday of the month, Divina told him to stop coming over. He never listened, and she always had a large meal prepared. It was a tradition built in wet sand waiting for the rain to destroy it. Until then, the two would dance around the ritual as if it were a religion. "I see him! I see him!"

Belinda gave Mary a quizzical glance and said, "That's preposterous. It's just a shadow." Mary let her lungs push out the excited air. She knew soon a shadow would belong to John.

Visitors were few and far between these days. Winter was even worse. Months could go by without a word, without a whisper. At least in summer, people would get lost and find their way there. The children were young, and the ladies were on constant watch. Strangers brought news of the world. News that could not be contained in old papers. They told wild stories of places and people, events and extraordinary miracles that made eyes open wide and jaws shake with wonder. John was not as exciting as foreign beings with strange clothes and thick accents, but he brought an element to the place.

"Belinda, I told you! There he is," Mary exclaimed with animation.

"You thought he was a shadow that appeared five minutes ago, Mary." Mary shook her head.

Belinda peered and squinted harder. "Ah, yes. There he is."

Divina watched the women in their flustering poses. They were like pigeons that had been feeding quietly and were disturbed by a fast and furious motion. Both turned in perfect unison to pierce Divina with their eyes.

"Straighten your dress," Belinda ordered as she walked over to do it for her.

Mary wheeled herself after Belinda and beckoned Divina to bring her face down to her own. Then, Mary licked her finger and erased a dot of batter from Divina's cheek.

"Gross," Claude observed.

Divina shrugged it off. The two women were already halfway to the front door. Claude gazed after them, and he didn't bother to hold back a yawn. John's voice was polite and clear as the ladies flocked over him. Divina knew that this was always the longest night of the month.

John's stride was exaggerated and practiced. The two women cowered around him like an alter. Mary never kept her hands off him. She was tugging at his shirt or using her spit to remove dirt or patting him on the face when he sat down. Tonight, John was more rushed than usual. Scrubbed and glowing, he usually cleaned up very fast and well after a day at work. His hands were tan, but for once, residue clogged the shimmering of his fingernails. Dust and golden strands of plant were embedded in his slicked back hair. Divina managed a sincere glance at him, one that brought color to her face and washed away the gritty feeling in John's throat.

"Good evening, Divina," John said as he walked over to her and kissed her on the cheek.

"Have a seat, John. Supper's almost ready," she replied as she quickly moved away from him. Her hips swayed as she glided to the other side of the kitchen. John had just started with this kissing custom as a greeting, and it made her terribly uncomfortable.

She didn't know where to place her hands. The air in her lungs moved toward her throat at an immense pace, choking her. She wanted so badly to be a child again.

Belinda and Mary took their places at the table. John had his own designated seat. The chair that called itself his was not removed from the table anymore; it sat empty except for the few times when he attended dinner. The boys crawled and mumbled until food was set on the table. Claude and Edgar then went through a magical transformation. They did every month. Guests, even if it was only John, called for manners and actions of perfect gentleman. The family would never easily forget to practice in case of company.

The smell of meat and potatoes filtered through the window and traveled outdoors. Windows were propped open with splintered pieces of wood. Laughter erupted easily from the table. None of the china matched, but each plate and cup and dish had a history, a beauty. The boys' words were stronger and held more weight. Another man in the house was a welcome change. Supper lasted an hour, and when it was over, the dishes were piled on the counters. Belinda and Mary did them whenever John ate with the family. Divina begged them not to because it meant she would have to entertain John until he left. That was precisely why the women acted as they did.

"Let's go outside," John suggested to Divina as she rose from the table.

A hundred good reasons not to go outside flooded through her mind. She nodded in agreement with a plastic smile playing across her face.

The evening had cooled down the day's torrid heat. Songs of rustling trees cornered the house. Night was beginning to fall, and Divina knew it would be easy to convince John to leave soon. She planted herself on a clear spot on the massive stairs. Scratching a bug bite on her ankle unconsciously, she cleared a place for John to rest beside her. He came closer than she meant.

"Stop that," he said, referring to her violent scratching.

She shot him a glare. "How's Edgar doing at work?"

"He's great, a very hard worker."

She shook her head in quiet protest at his blatant lie. Her arms came up around her, she hugged her knees, and she eased her chin on her hands. Rocking softly, her snowy fingers spread the small gush of blood to their tips from the insect bite. Barely noticing, her legs moved just enough to remove the fabric of her mother's dress from near the liquid.

"That's disgusting," John said to her.

"Sorry," came her reply without a hint of remorse. She wondered if he thought she was trying to be repulsive to him, and then she wondered if maybe she was actually doing so without truly thinking about it.

"It's going to be one of those nights," he observed.

"What kind of night are you talking about?"

"A dark night with no moon. Will you be all right? Do you want me to stay?" His tone was too hurried, too expecting.

"Nights are typically dark, John. I've been through enough of them; there's no need for you to stay."

"Are you sure?" She didn't look at him. His eyes would be too pleading. "I suppose I should go then, before it gets too dark to find my way," he stated.

The truth was that she knew all too well that he could find his way in the dark. It gave her a reason to let him leave, so she jumped all over it. If she let him stay one night, then there would inevitably be more nights. The rain would stop him, or the heat, or various other unseen reasons. He already had carved himself into dinners. "Good night. I'll talk to you again soon," she politely said.

John turned as he left; he always did. She often waved from the window, or the boys would walk with him until they reached the thicker brush.

Tonight she did not linger her gaze on him. He hesitated only a few seconds when he saw that she had already erased him from her thoughts.

She settled herself with the sky. The night was terrifying. The resemblance was undeniable. The clouds parted, the sun had melted, and goose bumps punched through her skin. A single breath brought her right back to so many years ago.

* * * * *

It was a black night in the summer. There were no stars that night. It was a celebration. Claude was being born! The house was alive, full of motion. Outside the walls, it was infinitely different. Stillness reigned over the air. Blades of grass didn't even dare to lean to one side. Edgar was tiny then, scrawny. His bones thrashed in an effort to break free from the thin covering of skin. The world was new and shiny to all of the inhabitants of the house.

Mr. Hamilton had called for a doctor. His wife's rush of sudden pain had prohibited them from traveling the long distance to the hospital. Mary ran through the house, which was lit up like a Christmas tree. Divina was barely a young lady, more on the verge of the end of childhood. She stood, not quite tall enough to reach the higher kitchen cabinets without climbing on the counter. She turned on the faucet, and the holy waterfall soaked into the old fabric pieces. Her footsteps were clean and breaking, each plastic dress shoe snapping against the wooden floor as she rushed to her mother's side. Rebecca was calm, trying not to show fear. Divina would place the cool rags gingerly on her mother's forehead. Rebecca would reach out, take her daughter's hands in a effort to say thank you. It was not as if she had never given birth before.

Mr. Hamilton's father was there, quiet and shadow-like. Edgar stalked him, watched him like he was a thief. Edgar was his shadow, lurking behind every corner bitten by curiosity and pride, loyalty and suspicion. He didn't visit often, didn't send gifts like their mother's relatives whom they had never seen. Rebecca was still an outsider, a muse for his son who was waiting for the right woman. Years had wrestled his life away as he watched the two of them drown into an ocean, dragging accidental children down with them.

Divina was her mother; Mr. Hamilton knew this right away. The deep black pupils were distressed, hopeful, full of her mother's essence. Divina, since birth, wanted to see everything, learn about the unknown, touch all that was around her. Rebecca cherished her, brushed her hair, and told her stories of France on rainy nights. Singing in angelic proportions, Rebecca found her daughter to be eager about everything she did. Literally, the child walked in her footsteps, followed her about the house, spoke words with the same rhythm. The child walked with delicate strands of attachment, clear pools of blue eyes rippled with innocence, and cooing harmonic mumbles. The little girl barely left her parents, and when she did, it was only to play with neighborhood children. Mostly, John lived the closest and was the first she found as a suitable friend. If her parents were not completely twisted and tied together before, then they were now.

Rebecca didn't fall into the mother role; she was consumed by it. Her quiet life didn't seem so silent anymore. Divina clung to her, worshipped her. All that little girl needed was her mother. Mr. Hamilton worked late, worked hard, and tried his best to balance the shaking weights of fatherhood and working. He would take her to the fields sometimes, to his office other days. Questions poured out of her, big giggles and silly expressions. Every night when he returned to the house, Mr. Hamilton would check in on his baby girl, his wife, and stare at them sleeping. Hours can easily be lost in such a mystic ritual. Divina's breaths were so perfect and timed, his wife's so soft and feminine. Their legs and arms would twitch in dream, and he'd part their wild hair and kiss the white line of their scalps before slipping off into an exhausted sleep of his own.

Edgar burst into this world with a sly gleam in his eyes. Rebecca expected another version of her daughter, but Edgar refused to acknowledge their preset expectations. The boy was sullen, isolated. His thoughts fell over him, drifted past the reality of childhood and into the realm of imagination. Hidden spots and shadowy buildings called to him. Rebecca had to chase him down as her daughter clung to the hem of her summer dresses. Mr. Hamilton would say it was just as well--boys will be boys. Edgar was doing what was natural, male, masculine. The boy was always reaching for what was too far away from his stretched fingers. His father thought it was a good sign implying the boy would try to do impossible things.

With a third child on the way and in a hurry, Mr. Hamilton had his worries. Neither he nor his wife were as young as they used to be. Rebecca wore her youth like an old shawl. Both knew that this would be their last.

Rebecca had been sick for a while. It was too early to be in labor, but Claude didn't care. He knew what he wanted, and he was ready to come out into his new world.

"Divina," a big breath was lost in the whisper, "go and find your brother." She felt her face strain against the inner turmoil but kept her mouth moving. "Maybe the two of you can find a middle name for this little guy," Rebecca said, fighting anything that may scare her daughter.

Mr. Hamilton looked on, backed by Mary and a doctor who had just arrived. He motioned for Divina to scurry out of the room. Divina was an old professional in her own mind; she had already helped her mother with one child. Now, she was a practiced helper.

The hall was filtered by lights that couldn't hold shadows. The door to the bedroom where her mother rested was shut tight but illuminated by the brilliance of the tweaks of light that escaped from the frame. Rainbow white beneath the door and through the keyhole made all other light dim. Edgar was in a room further down the house, hidden patricianly by a red velvet curtain overlooking a chair on which his grandfather sat reading an old bound Bible. Divina entered the room as she heard commotion coming from behind her. As she turned to go back, Mary thundered toward her, blocking her path of the hall.

Grabbing Divina's shoulders and turning her, walking her back in the opposite direction of Rebecca, Mary, in all sincerity, muttered, "It was nothing. Go find your brother. And get some more cold rags."

Mr. Hamilton was clenching his wife's hand, wiping the river of sweat from her forehead. Hair matted to her rosy cheeks. Rebecca tried her best not to scream but lost the battle several times. Muscles contracting, red liquid crawling toward her via the white comforter, and piercing hooks inside her tore off pieces of flesh from the inside out while her body convulsed. Worried husband eyes saw her leave before the doctor did, felt her float up above them, and gently brush the top of his hair. The beating vessel was filled with her daughter, her boys, her life, and it held too much to continue its frenzied beat. Softly whistling a lovely song, the moon suddenly gave light and a new breeze from an open window exploded from the dark for a brief moment to release her. Claude, tiny and sick, coughed and cried as his voice entered her ears. Mr. Hamilton knew she heard the baby, but before she could touch him, look at her husband, even acknowledge happiness, she was gone.

26

Belinda had been awakened by her sister. She flew in a bound rush down the stairs, through the room in which the children sat, and down the hall. Divina had watched in awe, her aunt naked of her usual jewelry. Fear had set in her cheekbones. Belinda had come to visit not long ago. She was the only one from Rebecca's family who ever came.

The doctor took the baby with him; Mr. Hamilton followed behind. Mary and his father looked at them, her eyes pleading, his asking in a stoic stare.

To this day, Divina does not know how she was told, if she was told. Her body felt it, as did Edgar's. All she could muster was to peer after the wet child who cried in a whimper. She remembered Claude coming home a few days later and being told that he had a heart condition. Her grandfather left suddenly, slid out the door, and she never saw him again. The old man, she heard, moved to a place by the ocean, and drifted out with the waves one night. She never asked about him; he was not a welcome subject. Divina never wanted to feel like she was a mistake, and that man could push that into her head with a mere look.

In less than a week, Mr. Hamilton had been back working in the fields. It was a strange cold afternoon with the kind of breeze that rips through clothes and adheres to skin. The sky was overcast with the gray blanket of grief. Work didn't overtake his mind on this day, and his thoughts betrayed him. With a loss of concentration, he made one mistake. It was over quickly. John's father found him, wrapped in a machine that had gotten the better of him. Divina only knew that he had been in an accident. Belinda and Mary took on the responsibility of the children with a vengeance that rivaled the commitment of their parents.

Chapter 3

Divina snapped back to life, and with a breath of evening air, she centered herself and entered the house. The dishes were done, and glossy eyes waited anxiously for juicy tidbits of her conversation with John.

"So, how is John tonight," Belinda asked with a hint of sweetness etched in her words.

"He's fine. We didn't speak about anything, and he's already home by now," Divina answered to the women who stared after her as she left the room. Pulling the blankets up over her head, Divina sunk into the old mattress. The lids of her eyes stung, refused to let sleep swim with them. It was early yet, and the silent shadow reached over the blankets, tugged at them in protest.

"Are you ill?" Edgar's voice cloaked her eardrums in concern.

"I'm fine, just a little tired."

"Do you want me to get you anything," he asked in a shaken attempt to take care of her for once.

"No," she answered as she sat up and brushed her hair behind her ears with her hands. He turned to go. "How was work today," she asked quickly.

"Same as always. We got a new guy today, foreign I think. Seems cool."

"You can go, it's all right," she said to his uncomfortable look at their attempt at decent conversation. His eyes darted across the floor, and she crawled back into her den of cotton.

When morning came, she found a glass of water placed by her bed and some crackers. A simple gesture, it filled her and reminded her that things were fine.

The kitchen called her, as it did every morning, to prepare Claude's medicine and make breakfast. A stranger was there today. It had been months since a stranger had been in the house, and she hadn't realized it. The deep accented voice traveled down the hall to her room, went through her covers, and emptied itself in her barren wasteland of thoughts. She pulled on her work clothes, drab rags years old, older than her brothers and older than her years of life. Tying her hair back with a piece of elastic, she walked slowly to seize the voice on her journey to the kitchen.

The table was full. Edgar was at the head of it, proud and adult. He spoke with clarity, with deep and long sentences. Her eyes poured into him, into the man of the house that he had never been before. Next to him was the stranger, intoxicating and consuming. Dark brown skin and the liveliest eyes she had seen in a long while. Divina studied him, not finding him attractive at first glance, his face too lined as if chiseled out of stone, as if drawn with a pencil. Everything about him at first glance was indented and perfectly straight. His voice was thick and harbored a small Spanish accent, and his English was perfect, the words melting together in mumbled conversation like merging worlds. She knew well that there was nothing mundane with newness.

"Good morning," Divina greeted the room. Faces came to her full attention. Claude sat on the floor, and Belinda leaned against the counter taking in the stranger from a distance. Mary had wheeled right next to him of course, too close for comfort, but he seemed fine.

Edgar's eyes were not distant like they often were, but he was alert and strength erupted from him. His smile was contagious; everyone at the table was wearing it.

"Good morning," the stranger replied.

"This is Marc," Edgar introduced him.

"Nice to meet you," Divina said as she kept her eyes glued to him in fascination. She hadn't seen a new face since the last time she had headed into town. Lately, John had been running all of her errands for her, so she hadn't been away for a few weeks.

"He's the new guy John hired," Edgar said.

The stranger, Marc, extended his hand. Divina shook it with a polite grip. She noticed his fingernails, singed at the very tips and exuding an odor of matches. The blackened line was dense, colorful against the tan yet white nails. It made her curious, made her wonder about how that came to be.

Divina quickly put aside her silly girlish questions, the ones that popped in her mind at the sight of the new face. As a child, she asked them, and as an adult, she had learned it was best not to say such abrupt words to strangers. Some people mistook the curiosity for something else, for some sort of prying into places which even those closest to the strangers had never ventured, never seen, never known existed. Divina had guts, piercing and bloody, and she did not live the life of a meek, quiet female. She had learned, however, an art to her madness as when to let judgment decide and when to speak when her mouth commanded. This was a cautious time, a time of judgment.

"The sun is barely up," she said as she passed Edgar, flowing her hand over his hair. "You'd better eat something before you go out for the day."

"I made some eggs. We've already eaten. I've been the proper master of the house to our *guest*," Edgar answered her, dragging out the word "guest" as if it were a joke upon itself. The guest was obviously seen as more of a casual friend than a newcomer who needed royal treatment.

Divina's mouth plummeted open. She could not retrieve her jaw in time for it to not be noticed. Edgar never made breakfast. This was a historic feat.

"She's right; we'd better go," the stranger, Marc, said as he stood up.

Belinda told the room, "John must be busier than we usually think, hiring a new employee and asking Edgar to work more hours during the week."

"He is," Edgar answered as he started towards the door.

Before Edgar could grab Marc and make them disappear, Marc looked back in at the room full of people. "It was nice to meet you all. Hopefully, I'll get to know you better soon." With that, their shadows vanished behind them out into the dawn.

Belinda yelled after them, "Come to dinner tonight! The both of you! And bring John! Divina will make something grand!"

Divina threw Belinda an annoyed glare but burst out laughing. "I'll make something good, huh? You volunteered, you cook."

The room stopped when Belinda answered, "Fine." Divina did not remember a time when Belinda had made a meal for the whole of them.

"I have work to tend to," Divina said as she scurried out of the house. The air hit her like a wave of water, boiling water, but water nonetheless. Today she would work near the house, in the backyard, on the garden.

Midmorning soon approached and passed: An odd day, to say the least. Mary wheeled herself out onto the porch overlooking Divina. In the different battles of light bouncing off the vegetation, the house, the windows, both women seemed at times old, at other times children. It took Divina a while to notice that Mary was outside. She instantly took a break and joined her on the porch.

"This shade is heaven," Divina said as she sat down on the steps near Mary's wheelchair. She slid a cuffed sleeve down and wiped her forehead and the indent above her top lip.

"It is a beautiful day," Mary said in a far off tone.

Divina knew there was some reason Mary had come out during the hottest part of the day. It had to be important.

"Mary, what is it?" Divina leaned over, touched her hand to Mary's. Mary's flesh was wrinkled, too soft, and it almost felt as if it would slide right off into Divina's fingers.

Mary dug into the space on the side of the wheelchair. An envelope, opened and fairly weathered read, appeared in her hands. She handed it to Divina without eye contact. The pain in her face was fierce; she couldn't look at the loved one who sat beside her. Divina opened it carefully as if it might bite her.

"I'm sorry," Mary said, her voice caught on some emotion, quivering. She closed her eyes in the fear that seeing would break her, would break the fragile covering that kept her of this earth.

"Oh, God," Divina whimpered, her hand clasping over her lips as her eyelashes fluttered and held back denial which wished to be set free. Slowly, she placed her arms around Mary as she held herself up onto her knees. Divina placed her arms gingerly, not wanting to hold on too tightly, but she crushed anyway as Mary let a single tear fall.

Mary was crying more for them than for herself.

"You are the only one I have told," Mary said as she began to gain control of the moment.

Divina looked deeply at this woman who had been there for the majority of her life. Her eyes narrowed, bit into her eyelids.

"It is all right, Child. Nothing can be done," Mary said soothingly, purring like a kitten to ease the pain out in the open.

"No," Divina said as she got up, angry and determined. She pulled in a breath, pulled one in so tightly that Mary reached out to touch her. Divina backed away, full of defiance. Her road was clear now, paved and shining despite being littered by rain. She knew what she had to do now because in that moment, all the choices vanished and withered away like leaves in fall. All that was left was this.

"Divina--"

"Don't worry, Mary. Everything's going to be fine. I am going to fix this."

"Divina!" Mary yelled at her as Divina turned to go inside, dead as stone, a stoic emptiness crawling into her expressions.

A few minutes later Divina emerged from the house again, dressed in her mother's white dress, one with such beauty that Mary almost forgot the severity of the situation. Divina reached over and stroked Mary's hair.

"You don't have to fix anything. You can't."

"I will do this for you, Mary. I love you, and I'll see you when I get back," Divina said.

"Please, Divina, don't..."

Divina tattooed a smile on her lips for Mary, and she began to walk towards the thicker brush. Mary watched her go, holding in her hand the letter which stated that Mary wasn't doing as well as the doctor's had said not so long ago. Mary was sick, the kind of sick that destroyed not only the person with the sickness but those surrounding as well. And as much as Mary understood that she had lived a long life, and it was her time to go, Divina could never understand. All Divina knew was that she could not lose another person she loved.

Divina reached John's vast farm quickly. Her hair had been brushed, her face washed and painted. John was entering the large home he built. The phone had rung. He got off the business call by the time Divina had reached his door. Edgar was in a shed nearby completely oblivious to his sister's presence. Marc alerted him to it by dropping a hammer and staring.

"Who is that?" Marc looked to Edgar for an answer. Edgar glanced and answered with his sister's name and then went right back into work. Marc stared after her, amazed at the transformation.

"Come on, you have got to be kidding me," Edgar said to Marc when he noticed the interest.

"It is just that, well... I mean, this morning she looked like... no offense."

"A dirty peasant?"

"No," Marc said sharply. "Don't talk about your sister like that."

"Then don't look at my sister like that." They both broke into a grin and shook their heads. A level of understanding had just been formed. Divina was no longer a subject to be reckoned with.

"Back to work," Marc said.

Edgar dug right back in, but not before harboring a longer glance at Divina. Something was up. He looked back at Marc, whose eyes still remained on her, and they both returned to the machinery.

John burst through the door and smiled as he looked at Divina. "Wow, you look fantastic. To what do I owe this?"

Divina tried her best to smile at him, hoping he wouldn't see right through her.

Edgar finally threw down his tools. "Let's just go get it over with," he said to Marc as if the only way to be polite would be to go and greet Divina when really it was more curiosity that drew them away from their work.

They both walked out, and Marc shook his head seriously, saying, "Formalities."

As usual, Divina didn't have to wait long for the quip that always came from John. "So, are you staying," John asked her even though he knew what she would say. It was more unwritten rules of conversation. He put himself through it every time although she often wondered why he never gave up.

"You mean, am I staying for dinner," she asked him.

"Well, actually, I meant forever, but dinner is good."

At this point, Divina always rolled her eyes and said something along the lines of dinner is all he'll ever get, to which he would reply dinner would satisfy him until tomorrow when he would wake up yet another day older and still without her.

Then, she'd tell him, well, you'll have me a little while longer if you make something really good for desert. Oh, and if you break out the wine, then hell, I may not be home until the latest hours permissible to still seem a demure and respectable young lady.

He'd laugh and tell her that she had forgotten he knew her too well for that. She would never be a demure young lady in his eyes. She was far too devilish to be considered an angel.

On this night, these words were not spoken, and things would never be as they were a moment ago.

Just as Marc and Edgar reached hearing distance, Divina said, "Yes."

John had worry fly across his eyes, and he stumbled. "What do you mean?"

As permanent an expression as on the figure that makes a fountain, her facial emotions did not change.

"Yes. To both. Dinner and forever."

"That is not funny," he said scolding her. He knew damn well she knew how he felt about her. In all the years gone by and despite how many times he said it, it was always something she couldn't say.

"I woke up today. To life. I am not a little girl anymore. What can I say to convince you, John?"

"Out of the blue," he asked with skepticism.

"Look at me."

"I have for quite a few years," he said with a meek laugh.

"I am raising two children and taking care of the others in the house. By myself. I have always had you to count on, my one rock. But I live my life alone."

"Divina, you know you don't have to marry me. I will always be there. Don't marry me just because you think you are alone. You know in your heart that you are not alone. As long as I live, you never will be. We can just forget about this whole thing," he said. He gave her the out he thought she had been looking for.

"Are you taking your proposal back?"

"I guess I am," he answered seriously.

Divina drew in a breath. "Fine. You want me to earn this." He looked at her with almost sadness in his eyes. He wasn't sure what he was doing or thinking. "John," she said as she got down on one knee, "will you marry me?"

He stared at her. He felt like his chest had been ripped open so many years ago. She had his heart, dragged it around with her throughout the years of childhood, through the trauma, and the dirt, and the woods, through the fights and the friendship. Now, she had placed it back in his chest, a piece of her inside the big hole he carried around in the biggest part of the valves.

Then, she said it. Well, she almost said it. "I need you, John." It was close enough.

"Are you serious? You're going to marry me," he asked in awe and with a hint of skepticism.

"Don't say it like that," she said and accidentally broke into a real smile. She knew he didn't believe it yet.

"You love me. You are going to be my wife," he said as he took her hand and kissed it before taking her into a large hug.

Edgar and Marc stared and barely found any sense in the words they had just heard. "No way. This is insane," Edgar said under his breath. Only Marc heard him.

"I didn't know they were..." Marc said to Edgar.

"Me either," Edgar replied incredulously. "If you would have asked me five minutes ago, I would have said they weren't."

John said, "Oh, this is the greatest thing that has ever happened to me. I knew you'd come around. I knew you were the one. I love you so much."

As she finally put some pressure in her arms around him in their hug, she simply said, "I need you."

"I love you," he said as he kissed her all over her face with tiny bird kisses. She replied nothing. "You're going to marry me," he said with excitement and a hint of question.

Finally, she spoke again. "Yes, I am going to marry you."

He released her and looked at their audience. "Meet my fiancée," he stated. Edgar stared at the two of them in shock. A moment passed in silence with awkward stillness. John's arm wrapped around Divina's shoulders with such possession. Divina weakly lifted her arm to cross John's back. She was shaking. Edgar searched her face, and she could tell he wanted to mouth the word "why" to her.

Marc finally broke the cloud air and said, "Congratulations. You have yourself a beautiful woman there. If we could all be so lucky."

Marc and John shook hands, strong and tough and maybe with too much ferocity. "Come in," John said to his employees. "It is a call for a celebration!" John ran into the house to find Cook and tell him a feast was in order. Tonight they were going to rejoice and drink and enjoy the happiness of company. Divina walked in behind him; Edgar ran to catch up with her. His eyes filled up when he looked at her.

She took his shoulder in her hand and said, "It's all right, Edgar. Be happy for me. Everything is going to be fine."

"You've lost your mind," Edgar said. He eyed her like she had grown a second head.

"Be happy for me," she repeated pleadingly.

John ran about from window to window, yelling for all to come inside. They were breaking out the good champagne, the oldest wine. Everyone was to come and drink, come and join this festive occasion. John, finished with running around like a chicken with its head cut off, returned to Divina's side. John turned to Edgar, waiting for some burst of acknowledgment on the news.

Edgar fulfilled this expectation by wrapping his sister in a hug and saying, "Divina, I am happy for anytime in which you find happiness." As he pulled away, only Divina knew the extent of this message. The two hadn't hugged for years, and the boy she knew before her was now a man she barely recognized. He knew more about her than she gave him credit for because in that instant, she knew

Edgar had his suspicions. She also knew Edgar loved her, despite his lack of showing it, and he would never disrupt whatever she had just set in motion.

John didn't leave Divina's side for the rest of the afternoon and early evening. He drank while she didn't touch the alcohol although she made it seem as though she always emptied her glass. She answered when spoken to and laughed when it was called for. As the sky turned gray, she leaned in and put her head on John's shoulder.

"I should be getting back," she said to him.

"I'll come with you," he said as he sat up straight and was ready to leave. "We'll tell everyone the news together. They will be so happy you came to your senses."

"No," she said, too fast. "No, I mean, I should tell them. You have work to do, and you may have had a little too much to drink. You stay here, and you can see them tomorrow. Besides, I have to explain this to Claude."

John took this in and thought it a relevant excuse. He shook his head in agreement.

"Good," she said and kissed him on the cheek before he had a chance to grab her or ask her to stay or come back. She knew he was thinking it. She'd put it off until after she was married, and even then, she had time from now until that day to find an excuse. Right now, she couldn't harbor the thought of spending the night with him. He was like her brother or an estranged yet well-known cousin.

She left and didn't look at the lights that shined from his place behind her. When the noise from the party died down in her ears, she began to weep softly as she walked.

The trail was blackened by night, but she knew the way well from childhood. There was a blanket of insect song over the silence. The moon was half full, staring at her from its cracked lens. She could hear the twigs breaking under her feet. The rain of the saline from her eyes fell earth shattering.

"Are you all right," a voice exploded from the silence and broke it like it was melting.

"Who's there," she commanded as she spun around.

"It's just me, Marc. John sent me to--"

36

"I can find my way alone, thank you. You can go back now."

"No, he wanted me to give you this," Marc said as he appeared to her with the moon making shadows dance across his face. His voice was laced with disbelief. She took the object in her hand and studied it before breaking out into a laugh mixed with a sob. "Not very romantic, is he?" Marc asked her as he tried to make her smile.

"I don't think romance exists anymore anyway," she said as she wiped her face with her hand and hastily slipped the diamond on her finger. It was John's Grandmother's, a family heirloom he had shown her many times before. It was breathtaking, sparkling and winking at the darkness, reflecting the light of the stars. Simple, yet devastatingly radiant.

"You're crying," he said as he grabbed her hands from her face, his eyes laced with worry. He knew the country was hard, and she was just a mere girl. She could be hurt or bleeding from this brush.

"Must have been the alcohol," she said.

"You didn't drink any."

"Sure I did--"

"You did not. I was watching," he said as he smiled.

"Okay, so I am not an alcoholic. So, I drank water. Who cares?"

"Are you hurt? Did you cut yourself running through the forest?"

"No, I am fine," she said to him.

"Obviously not. Fine people don't cry."

"I'll be fine. I just need to go home and rest. You should be getting back."

"I can't just leave you like this. John wouldn't want me to go with you all upset and emotional." Her face squared as it often did when she protruded strength. "I can go get him," Marc said in an effort to be helpful.

"No," she said with an icy glare. His answer from her was chilling.

"I mean, he is your lover and you're marrying him, so you should be happier than this. I admit, I am dumbfounded. Those aren't the normal tears of joy."

Before she thought, sharpened words escaped from her mouth. "Lover! I am not his lover!"

The unexpected answer made his eyes widen. "Of course not," he answered quickly. "I forget, you know, being from the big city. In places such as this, it is customary to wait. Please forgive me." Her reddened face showed even through the night. "I didn't mean to embarrass you," Marc said.

And it was true. Even in such modern times, communities such as this were small and sweltered with gossip. Morals and religion were learned from an early age. Even if you didn't believe what you were taught as a child when you came of age, you knew the toll your choices would take not only on yourself but your family.

"It is all right. Pay me no mind," and she added for his benefit and belief, "I am just a silly girl. Good night."

She turned then to leave, and he watched as she disappeared in the brush. Her movements were perfect, and he instantly saw that she had done this a million times. He thought she belonged in the cat family with tigers and lions because her back arched just so underneath branches. He didn't follow her, but knew now that he had fallen into a place with deep-rooted history and banished secrets. Nothing would be simple here; this he understood now. She had sounded as if she despised this man who she practically proposed to a few hours ago. In fact, she seemed to be weeping over the pain of being with him. Her own brother was surprised. If she wasn't marrying him for love, then why was she marrying him? As he put his feet into his past footsteps to make his way back, he told himself this was none of his business. It was best to leave this alone.

Divina reached her home and went into the kitchen. An addicting smell covered her with such force that she yelled, "Belinda?"

Belinda came quickly as if she were only a room away. Her face was stern and disciplined, but it changed to worry when her eyes settled on Divina.

Divina had forgotten Belinda had promised to cook dinner tonight, and what a dinner it was! Food poured over the counters and on the table; the dishes were clean and shining. There was fruit from the garden garnishing pies and cobblers and meats. It looked as if a great bird had been prepared for weeks for this splendid occasion. It looked wonderful and smelled as if tasting it may hinder the greatness of the food.

Divina fell into a chair as Mary wheeled close to the kitchen to see what all the commotion was. Claude was toddling near her. "What is it, honey," Belinda asked as she took a seat next to Divina.

Divina just put her head in her hands and let the crying go for a moment, let it take her over and shake her shoulders without rhythm. She gained her posture after a second of loss, found her strength that made her the rock in this house.

"You're marrying John," Belinda said as if she knew the answer but couldn't believe it. Even she recognized the ring on Divina's finger. It glowed glittery before Belinda's eyes.

Claude's mouth dropped open as Divina shook her head to show that she had found the truth in her grief. Claude ran over and jumped into Divina's arms.

"Why," he asked her while searching his brain for a reason he must have missed. He was young, but he had heard the stories of love about his parents' and relatives' loves. The two old women were always telling stories of great romance.

"It was meant to be," Divina said as she faked a smile. Her eyes felt hollow as did the inside of her skin.

"People marry to be happy, right?"

"Yes, Claude. John makes us happy. He's a nice man who will take care of us. You can go to school."

Claude's eyes lit up at the possibility. Then, another thought occurred to him and played over his face. "Then, why are you crying?"

"Sometimes people cry when they are happy."

"But you look sad."

"I am fine, Claude. I love you very much, right?"

"Yes," he said as if he didn't understand where this was going.

"And whenever you wander off and get lost, what do I do?"

"You cry because you are scared. Are you scared to marry John," Claude asked helpfully as if this he could understand.

"And then, I cry harder when we find you, right? Why is that?"

"Because you're so happy!"

"You got it!"

Claude smiled in understanding, and then he started reciting the alphabet. He was ready for school. Divina hadn't known how she was going to send him. She thought she would figure something out because she always did. And in a way, she knew she had.

"It's getting late," Belinda said as she took Claude from Divina. "It is time for a little boy to go to sleep."

"Night, Mary," Claude yelped as he joyfully squirmed away from Belinda and bounded towards Mary. He kissed her hand because a year ago she had told him that is what gentlemen do. In reality, it was because he hurt her too much when he jumped up on her lap to kiss her cheek.

"I'll be in soon to tuck you in," Divina called after Claude.

Mary and Divina watched the little boy and Belinda leave the room, and then their eyes met. Everything was silent in the space between them. A moment passed with the two still searching each other. Divina finally rose from the chair and gathered herself into the motherly role to which she had been assigned years ago.

"Goodnight. I love you, Mary," Divina said as she kissed the top of the old woman's head.

"I know," Mary answered her just before Divina was out of hearing distance.

Claude fell asleep squirming with thoughts of children, of playgrounds, of the places he had only seen in pictures, only learned of from the books Divina read to him.

Divina knew as she took one last, long look at her little brother that the two old women were waiting for her in the kitchen. She sucked in a breath and straightened her back. Then, she walked strong and proud down the hall.

She reached the kitchen, and both women were staring at the doorway long before she had even appeared. Divina put her hands on her hips. Unfortunately, these women were the only people who knew her well enough to see through her.

"Mary told me," Belinda said, referring to the letter and the illness. Divina leaned against the counter. From her elbows to her wrists, her skin worshipped the cool marble. She let her weight fall upon it. "You don't have to do this. So rash, child. We'll figure something out; we always do," Belinda said soothingly.

"John won't be that upset if you tell him right away," Mary added urgently.

"I am going to say this once," Divina said to both of them. They waited, unsure what was coming. "I love him," she said.

Belinda's face slowly broke open into a smile eventually bringing tears to her eyes. Her face told the world that she had known this fact all along.

Mary trusted Divina with all things. Divina had never lied, would never lie. So, she had to believe her. Mary reached out for Divina who gave her a gentle embrace.

"Then, that is that," Belinda said. She didn't let out too much joy in her words or face, but she felt the relief like a shower rushing over them all, cleaning the previous issues as if Divina would have decided this even if

40

Mary had never shown her the letter.

"It is late. You should get to sleep," Mary said to Divina.

"Go ahead," Divina answered, giving Mary a gentle push out the door. Belinda followed behind Mary as Divina went towards the food.

Alone at the big wooden table, Divina dug through the piles of food that had been put away in the refrigerator and in the cupboards. Her head felt too heavy for her body.

She picked at a piece of fruit, some dark color with a fuzzy peeling. Her limbs were so shaken that she couldn't hold the fruit still long enough to decide what it was. Not that it mattered. She couldn't taste anything either. Taste buds were sandpaper, scratchy and corrosive. Her throat felt nothing as she swallowed down the fleshy pieces of fruit.

Today, she thought to herself, I did not lie. And she knew this to be true. "I do love him," she whispered for no one to hear. In her head, the words came too fast for her to censor them, to stop them. It was the kind of thought that you tell yourself you will not think because if you don't acknowledge it, then surely your motives are as pure as you tell yourself they are.

The thought that plagued her too quickly, the one that would never fully leave her, drifted in her voice in her head this one time, this one time only before marriage. "But I am not *in love* with him."

Although there was no anger in her voice, no regret within her palms, she laid her head on her crossed arms on the table. The old wood scent drifted in her nostrils until there was nothing left but that smell. Only her mess of hair was visible, and if she had been able to see herself, she would have noticed immediately the shade of black falling over her head identical to her father's strands.

* * * * *

A crisp cool snapped at the dawn on that morning. Edgar was three years old. His hair and eyebrows were dark; his skin already tanned by the sun. The trees envied his ability to melt into the horizon. Even their branches stood out more than Edgar's limbs when viewed from a distance. In contrast to his sister's sky blue eyes, Edgar harbored a deep and secretive stare. Unlike his father whose eyes changed with emotion, Edgar's stayed that dark hue. It was as if he knew things others refused to see, let things in others kept out because of fear and pain.

41

Divina looked all of her nine years. Rebecca saw herself in her little girl while Edgar reflected only and all of Mr. Hamilton. Yet, when Divina scrunched her cheeks in concentration and curiosity at something around her, and her dark hair framed her face as if painted on in a picture perfectly, Rebecca could see the image of her husband. On this morning, the birds were singing, and Divina bounded alongside her mother, gazing lovingly at her. Rebecca watched as Divina scampered after Edgar in a rush of play. The girl's light skin and pale eyes were bright and ethereal. Today, Rebecca didn't recognize Mr. Hamilton in their children. In some twist, she was blind to the obvious connections.

"It's time," Mr. Hamilton said as he poked his head in the front door.

Rebecca was caught off guard, surprised by her husband's voice. It took her a moment to recognize it. She simply smiled weakly and nodded in agreement.

The children stopped stone cold. Their movements were still now as if they had been frozen in time. Divina then widened her gaze, as large as her eyes would open, hoping somehow if she looked at her mother hard enough, then her image would be burned into her mind. At nine years, she felt her mother's urgency, even her sadness.

She may not have understood it, but inside the feeling was there all the same. Edgar looked at her hard, searching without softness for some flicker of affection. His steps towards his mother were calculated, planned with immense concentration. Like a robot, when he reached where she stood, he wrapped his arms around one of her knees and hugged her quickly, stiffly at first. There was a brief, fleeting instant, though, when she felt his grip tighten, begging her for a mere second that she almost missed had she not been waiting for it, when he asked her without words not to go.

"I love you," Rebecca said as she reached down and stroked his dark hair. Her whole body felt about to fold when he smiled in acknowledgment. At last, he understood the words.

Divina waited for Edgar to let Rebecca go before she took a giant leap into her mother's arms. She tightened her hug around her mother's shoulders, so tight was her hold on Rebecca's hair that she flinched.

Rebecca gingerly placed her daughter standing on the floor in front of her.

"Come home soon," Divina said.

"I will," her mother replied honestly. Rebecca didn't linger long for fear she would change her mind. She gave a little wave before she opened the door. Then, she turned away from her children who watched as her shadow followed her away from them.

The gravel screamed in mercy beneath the cab's tires. The children bounded to the screen door, watched the yellow blur screech out of their vision. Mr. Hamilton stood in the cloud of dust left behind. It wasn't long before even the sound was gone and the residue completely still.

Mr. Hamilton stood there unmoving, watching the empty drive before him. As the tops of the trees swayed, his silhouette stayed immobile. It took Divina running into him at full speed to snatch him from his glazed over state. The children were outside now, and no matter how strong the pull was that pleaded with him to stay there staring, he knew inside he couldn't stand there a moment more with his children matching his stance. He wouldn't stay there and stare after her with them. No, he couldn't.

Rebecca had asked him to come along. She told him they could find someone to stay with the children. It would be just the two of them, like always, she said, together against the world. But he had work. It had happened so fast.

They had received the call on a mundane Tuesday afternoon. Rebecca's father had been in the hospital only a few months. The Hamiltons were going to go to him as soon as the harvest was over. He wasn't supposed to be in the last stages. No one had told them to prepare them. They hadn't known time was of the essence; they had been led to believe the exact opposite. Now, he was gone. As for his daughter, the one who never visited, who had a husband he had never met and children he had only known from pictures, she wasn't even there when he died.

Mr. Whitfield, Rebecca's father, was a stout and serious man. He thought his daughter knew about his condition. Her lack of contact surely meant a lack of caring.

With Rebecca's mother long buried, he had been one of the last immediate blood relatives.

After she heard the news and clearly saw her husband would not be joining her, Rebecca took a long flight and an even longer drive to reach her father. Somewhere inside, she felt her father could sense her presence although his human shell no longer held him of this world. As she placed him on the hill overlooking the water, with her mother, she felt his sadness over his mistake. His regret was evident as she, the refined French woman he had raised from birth, the girl who never jumped in puddles and was shocked by dirt, got down on her knees. The earth was soft, dark, and staining. Her hands dove deep into the ground. She planted the flowers, one by one, in the fertile soil. She knew because of her life now, because of her husband's wisdom, they would grow strong and flourish. The clouds rolled over her head, fast and furiously. Deep into the sunset she worked, and as she patted the last mound of dirt over the last seed, she let a tear fall. She stood, brushed her hands together and let the loose dust fall from her callused fingers. The stone was small, and the wealth the family had was not evident in its simplicity. She brushed off the soft layer of dirt that had gathered on the surface of the stone from the air.

"I forgive you, Daddy," she whispered to him with a sweet smile.

Somehow she felt he didn't mean it, this last stab against her. She tasted her trail of a tear, which fell down her cheek onto her tongue, and she knew he understood now.

He was weeping where he was, and he was all around her. This she felt. No matter how hard it may have been wished, the years were gone now.

She was no longer a little girl.

She was his daughter.

She had walked through the old house before bringing him here. The walls were the same eggshell white, the carpeting a rusty brown, the windows spotted near the sill.

Yet, the rest was gone. A colored torn fabric here, a fragmented dish there, or a cracked trinket were a few of the scattered remainders in a corner, in a cupboard, on a high closet shelf. He had used hand held scissors for the pictures, for her mother's paintings. The remains were a skeleton. He had taken the flesh from her memories. Pieces, fractured and streaked, were beyond mending. Because of his anger and resentment, he had left her nothing.

She forgave him not for him, but for herself. The things he had done to her were beyond repair long before this last will. She couldn't hate him anymore. She just didn't have the energy. Besides, she had been prepared for this. In fact, she had this all figured out before he did. She took action years before she took her first trip to the States.

Rebecca left her father there, knowing she would not return no matter how long she lived. Even in death, she had made it clear in her youthful years, she did not want to be reunited with her parents on that hill. Her life was no longer there. Some pains are better left alone.

Living out of her suitcase in the hotel room, Rebecca paced back and forth on this second night away from her family in New Orleans. The phone stared at her, daring her.

Despite herself, she still knew the number by heart. She walked over and picked up the phone.

She dialed the number quickly, rhythmically.

She rolled her eyes when a woman answered, the connection bursting with fuzz and static.

"May I please speak with Claude," she asked.

* * * * *

Divina sat at the wooden table in the kitchen long into the night. She drifted off many times but only for brief moments. Her body and mind were wide awake long before a decent hour in the new day.

The most unbelievable thing happened to her.

She greeted the new day with relief.

She was marrying John. To her own surprise, she felt a weight lifted from her, one so great and old that she had forgotten it had been hers for so many years. John had been giving her so much for her whole life, and now, she was finally going to repay him. He loved her. She knew she couldn't let him take care of her forever the way that he had been. It wasn't fair to either of them. Now, she was going to take care of him. And she knew if she was going to be a wife...

Wife. Divina bolted upright at that word coming to her thoughts. She hadn't comprehended the entire situation until now. She was marrying John. She was going to be his *wife*. Marrying John meant not a ceremony but a life. Motherhood. Goose bumps pierced through her skin, and she shook in the sudden revelation. I am twenty years old, she thought to herself. This time, it didn't sound young to her anymore. It sounded ancient. And she breathed it in as if she now owned the world.

She couldn't control everything anymore. The world was not as she saw it as a child; the world was not hers alone. It didn't matter what she thought she had wanted before because this wasn't about her. It was time to let it be about the people she loved. Her brothers, Mary, and even John, were the ones to concentrate on now. No more selfishness, she thought. Let's replace this all with happiness.

And then she started crying again, but these tears were not masked with the sadness. They were splashed with hope.

Chapter 4

"Who is it, Virginia," asked the voice from far away, approaching the phone. It was distinctly groggy, distinctly male.

"I don't know," the woman answered right into the phone without bothering to cover the receiver. "It sounds like they are selling something."

Rebecca heard the gruff grunt of distaste come from Claude as he put the phone to his ear.

"Yes," he barked loudly.

"Hello," Rebecca said softly, confidently. It would have been impossible to miss the tint of grief that fell over her tone. On the other side of the world, in a loft in New York City, Claude's light eyebrows arched up to the sky at the instant recognition of the voice on the other end of the line. He motioned the woman with him to leave; he was done with her for now. "My father died," she said to him, and it was all that needed to be explained.

Everything was understood. "I'll be waiting then," he answered. They both knew she would be knocking on his door within days.

Hair wild and tangled, Rebecca stepped off her latest flight. In the last three nights, she had slept ten hours total. Her body felt the exhaustion, but her mind raged. Sleep had forsaken her while weariness wore on every cell in her body. No matter how tired she was or how many times she closed her eyes with hours to spare, nothing gave.

She was back, though, in the only city that could accommodate her with such perfection. This was her city more now than it had been before, this city that never sleeps.

From plane to subway to cab, she stepped onto the sidewalk for the last leg of her trip. A black skirt fell past her ankles, swaying with her, mourning her movements. She crossed her arms around her waist, clutching tightly the deep navy blue jacket, keeping the body warmth from escaping into the streets. With one turn, she took a quick unexpected step into the side of a building. To the naked eye, one would not have noticed the small indent in the wall. She opened the hidden door with her key and began her journey up the flight of stairs.

Finally, when it seemed she would have to stop and catch her breath, the stairs ended. There were no more. The door seemed smaller now than she remembered, closer to the top of the stairs. The walk that used to take her an eternity now took her a few steps. Yesterday, she could barely remember. Now, it seemed as if it had happened not long ago.

Her gaze took it all in again, and despite the vagueness of her memories, the sight was just as magnificent. Once again, it had taken her and filled her, reminded her of the girl she used to be. She had not realized until now that person was a stranger, the one who lived in this city and answered to her name.

She didn't even have to knock at the door.

Claude had been watching her from the street. He sat on the ledge, the way they used to when they stared into the city lights on the dark evenings in the spring. He knew which subway she would take, which route she would give the cab driver. But he waited. Best to let her come into his world first instead of meeting her somewhere in the middle, somewhere they both shared but she still somehow owned.

He opened the door halfway, surprised at her aged face yet amazed at the remaining resemblance to old pictures. The premature lines around his eyes wrinkled softly, gently at the sight of her.

She had wanted to come up with some anecdote, a quirky line, a confident greeting. Now, she would have taken a few polite words. Unfortunately, she could not summon her mouth to open or her mind to let loose intelligent, charming words.

Before she could crumble in front of him, standing in the hall outside his door, without a word, he placed a hand on her shoulder and the other on her lower back, guiding her into the first few feet of his loft. She just fell into him, an awkward and strange embrace, shoulders shaking with the silent crying. One arm wrapped around her, he flipped the door shut quickly with the other in a movement with the right proportion to move his head next to hers. The comfort of touch fit them together. She leaned in, rocking back and forth, unable to stand straight up by herself. He planted his feet, tightened his muscles, and took on the weight as he stood balancing both of them.

* * * * *

The house became alive as the light peaked in through the dirty windows. The color of shade was enough to brighten the place. Divina had been in the attic for hours.

She figured it must have been years since anyone had ventured up there. It was a typical attic for an old house. There were boxes and shadows and spider webs. Divina was sitting on the floor in the midst of the mess. When she moved her legs or stretched to reach something, she left a mark on the floor because she had plowed through another part of the layer of dust covering everything. Her cough was loud and deep as she breathed in the swirling dirt. A gray swipe lined the apple of her left cheek, a disturbing darkness against her pale skin.

Box after box she opened, using her fingernails as knives to cut the tape. The sound was pleasurable, the ripping of the sticky fibers screeching when broken, letting her know the boxes were barely closed anymore. In she dug like a child at Christmas, greedy, searching for something she knew had to be there. Not realizing how fast and hard she was working, she drew in a short breath, gasping for air, when she at last saw the familiarity she had been searching for.

The painting.

* * * * *

After a moment, which seemed to last years, Rebecca regained her composure and backed away from the strong arms that held her. She wiped her eyes and put a slightly embarrassed expression on her face. Then, she looked about the room.

The loft was as she remembered it. A large rectangle, the entire place was one room: A bed in one corner, an easel in the middle, a small refrigerator and stove against an opposite wall. The ceiling was scattered with skylights, the glass reinforced with bars and gleaming brightly. Three walls were uniform white, white as snow and clouds and the surrounding of the colored circle in eyes. But one wall had changed, still as monstrous with color as it had been, but now with more movement and flow. The mural he had finished. She never thought she would see it done.

"Do you like it," he asked her.

She shook her head in awe as she turned toward him, taking in her first true look at him since the last time... Not wanting to set her eyes on him so fully, she darted her gaze away, then back, obviously staring and wanting to stop. She knew it was impossible. Was it really that long ago when she had told herself to memorize him, to tattoo him on her inner eyelids? I want to see you when I blink, she had told him.

Unframed painted canvases sat on the floor, held up by walls, piled in corners, even peaking out from under the bed. War colored swirls in battle and peace treaty scenic lands ranged from splashed paint without identifiable objects to vivid details as picturesque as a camera photograph. On a small sink, next to the faucet, in a mug where a dish sponge should be held, was a fistful of drying brushes.

There was an art piece, a reprint, nicely framed and hung high on a nail, the only piece actually placed on the wall. The place had been measured for this one thing to set off the rest of the disharmony in the placement of all other objects. It had been a gift from her before she had even really known him, before he understood her. Very famous and unlike his style, the cool colors of the water lilies rained over his wall. A Monet.

Rebecca looked at him now, in his eyes, and smiled without thought. Yes, they are still the same. The blue of his eyes still match that water under the lilies.

Claude hadn't changed much from college. His youthful glow and wide-eyed innocence was replaced by hardened lines, which still held kind indents. There was something bruised and steel where hope and belief had been. A determination in his hands, in his work, in his passion was still evident. Where in youth, he believed his destiny would be as great as the one who made the work she had given him on his wall, now, he knew better. What made him who he was still remained. He never stopped. Never.

The stormy blue of his eyes met hers as his interest matched her own. He was still taller, just a few inches, but she was rounder now. He knew instantly somehow she had come into motherhood. It surprised him. His hair was blond, falling perfectly as it did straight out of bed. No sun had touched his skin, no sun except from the skylights, but she was still paler. Enchanting perhaps. He could see her insomnia from the puffs under her lashes, and her hair, still as golden as the sun, was thinning and the residue begged to be kissed by rain. She had aged far beyond her years yet remained beautiful, and he wondered whether it had been gradual or all at once. And if all at once, did it happen recently, in the events that had brought her back here?

Dried paint on his white tee shirt and blue jeans, red and green flickers of color in his hair, the artist was alive in him still. Rebecca looked at him and thought it was no wonder his mother had named him Claude.

Chapter 5

Divina had surfaced from her long morning in the attic. It had been a week since the engagement began. John wanted to plan everything right away. Hurried and sure, he said there was no reason to wait. Divina didn't know if she had the right to argue especially since she couldn't think of any good reasons to postpone the ceremony. Luckily, Belinda came through for her.

John would have been happy to be married by a justice of the peace on the next idle Thursday. No need for a big, elaborate, expensive extravaganza. He was fine in jeans and a tee shirt. He had an "all we need is one witness" frame of mind.

Although it took Divina by surprise, she was hurt by this. Her mother and father had a tiny, secret ceremony of this exact sort. And they were happy, weren't they? She knew they loved each other and had lived a good life. Yet, in a spark of dream, she had imagined herself in a white wedding dress walking down an aisle. Childish, she shrugged these notions off. No reason to spend money on this of all things. It wasn't the ceremony but the time after it that was important.

Divina told John all of this, and Belinda overheard. *"Absolutely not!"* Belinda's voice registered shock when it boomed over the young couple.

"Belinda," Divina said, warning her not to speak without thinking.

"John, you aren't seriously considering this. She is going to wear a wedding dress. We are all going to dance. And, for God's sake, it is going to be in a church. A big church."

"A church is a good idea," John said to himself, obviously pondering these things.

Now, Belinda was off and running. "Lots of stained glass windows! We can have Claude be the ring bearer. We can have musicians--"

"This sounds mighty expensive," John interrupted.

"It is your wedding day. It's supposed to be expensive. Besides, we can cut some corners. I'll cook all the food," Belinda was off again.

"What do you think," John whispered to Divina. She looked at Belinda's excitement and laughed. Then, John looked at her seriously.

In the background, Belinda was still rambling. "We need to find a flower girl. Oh, and we have to find something blue, old, new, and some other thing I don't remember. Ah, yes! Borrowed! Maybe we need to get a bride book. Is there such a thing as a bride book? Bride magazines! That is a good idea..."

"We will do whatever you want," John said to Divina quietly. "You were never a girl who dreamed of being a princess, so I just kind of figured... I mean, if you want the works, then I am all for it. I just never really thought about it. This has always been about you and me in my mind, not a dress or a cake--"

"Oh, what kind of cake? White? Layered? I suppose it depends on how many guests," exclaimed Belinda who overheard the one word and was off in an entirely new frame of thought.

Divina broke through both of their little worlds when she said, "How about if we draw on middle ground?" The two opposite sides stopped and focused on her intently. "John and I won't run off by ourselves, but the wedding won't be over done."

Everyone smiled.

Divina thought of her parents. She had wanted the long dress and pictures and people. She set her eyes on John and felt a small sadness.

She remembered the last time she had locked herself in a small room upstairs, a tradition she did often as a child. A small, unnoticed smile bounced quickly off her lips when the memory returned to her. It had been only four short years ago, when she was sixteen. Or, maybe it was four long years ago. That was the last time she had danced, wistfully, waiting for her prince to come and bring her jewels of ruby and emerald. Anyone who would have walked in would have known. She was definitely, even if only in that room, a princess.

Once some of the details were decided upon, John headed back to his work. No live musicians. They would use prerecorded music. Dresses were outrageously costly.

Divina knew of some useless items in the attic that may be worth some money. She wouldn't buy the most expensive dress, although John would have paid for it. There had never been a time when she would have spent such money even for something she would get to wear more than once.

Surely, she thought, there will be a moderately beautiful one, and with a little searching, she could come up with a little money without John knowing.

Which led her to search the attic. She remembered the painting, a loud and seemingly unattractive piece. Her mother loved that painting, kept it in her private den.

Before Divina was born, and the house was full of wealth, Mr. Hamilton had given Rebecca a small room all her own. There she worked on her sketches, her architectural plans. This painting was some inspiration to her. Divina never liked it. It was rather messy and hard-featured. There were a few other old things she found while she searched, but the painting was the main thing she remembered. She figured it must be worth something if her mother treasured it so.

When she came upon it, she stared at it a long time, then brought it into her bedroom. She set it against a wall, unsure which way was up or down or sideways.

Divina kept many things her mother and father treasured and cared about. Keepsakes, clothing, pictures, and other things were placed throughout the house and in carefully guarded safe deposit boxes. This was one of those things Divina had never really wanted, and she was sure her mother wouldn't have been insulted. If she had lived longer, maybe she could have told Divina what she saw in the picture, and then Divina could see it, too.

* * * * *

"I am so sorry about your father," Claude said to Rebecca.

"Thanks," she answered, feeling a little silly at how much comfort she found in words, which did not bring comfort. It was merely his voice.

"I kept it all," he said quickly. "Despite it all, I never broke my promise."

"I know," she replied. Deep down, she had always known. That is why she had given him what she trusted with no one else.

"Doesn't seem that long ago, does it," he said, his thoughts coming through into words.

He knew she thought the same.

Rebecca had been young and on her first trip to America. She had been accepted to the school because of her sketches. When she arrived in the city, she had only planned on one semester abroad before she returned to France to finish her education. That was before people noticed how much talent she held. That was before Claude.

Rebecca had been on a date of all things. Years later, she couldn't remember the boy's name. She didn't remember if she had gone out with him before, where she met him, or whether she even liked him. Her date brought her up on the roof of a building, and attempting to show off, he guided her from top of building to top of building, showing her the city. She had been in New York for only a month or so. Passer-bys on the street yelled up at the two, which prompted them to climb down an old fire escape. It was too late for Rebecca. In one of the last fleeting moments above the city, specific shapes of a nearby building caught her eye. While she wasn't impressed with her daredevil date, he had peaked her curiosity, not in him, but in a sketch she dreamed of for three nights before venturing back to the fire escape.

Clad in pearls and silk floral fabric, she climbed higher and higher until she reached the top of the building. The rust from the fire escape left deafening marks on her shins and her dress. She didn't care. Her heels clicked and stomped on the roof until she sat at the perfect spot, just under the deepening shadows of evening. In an instant, she was sketching madly to capture it all.

Meanwhile, the stranger from below was awakened by the noise from above.

Birds definitely could not make such noise. He still had a few hours of sleep left in him before he rose in the night. Curious and worried, he decided to make sure everything was all right above him.

She was not from here; he knew this right away. Her ears didn't pick his approach up at all. He wasn't dangerous, but for all she knew, he could have been. Instantly, he disliked her, and when he saw the wealth written all over her, he disliked her even more. Wealth wasn't an asset to flaunt. Stupidity wasn't something you screamed either. This girl, it seemed, glowed with both those things.

Then, he came closer. So close, he could have touched her had he reached his arm out. His eyes flew on what was swallowing all her attention. She was drawing these buildings.

It was then she noticed him, jumping a little at the surprise of the company. He noticed there was no fear in her eyes.

"You know, you shouldn't be up here alone. It is dangerous," he said to her.

"Why? I can take care of myself. *You* aren't going to hurt me," she said knowingly. Her voice was defiantly adult. This stranger had no right to tell her where she could be as if she was a child. Her tone told him this, but it was in a way that was aimed toward an innocent as if he couldn't understand and was worrying over things he knew nothing about.

He opened his mouth, then shut it again. She watched him gather up fragmented sentences in his mind until he finally settled on one. Yet, he didn't seem to want to push, to say it.

"Go ahead, I can take it," she prodded.

"You are holding that wrong," he said, pointing to the charcoal with which she was drawing.

"What?" He bent down where she was and formed her fingers around the gritty blackness. It was awkward, both his touch and the charcoal. "You can't be serious. How would you know," she muttered, uncomfortable with the new position of her hand.

"Try it," he said with a tone so confident she recognized it as arrogant right away. Humoring him, she tried it. And he was right. The color flowed better, the shading was more precise. Slowly, she looked at him, somewhat mystified. "Come here," he said to her, taking her hand as she stood. They took a few steps together.

She looked down the nearest sky light into his loft. Now, she understood. His loft looked then as it did now, artistically messy. "Ah ha." Her eyes laughed, and her pose would make one think she had known all along even though she was genuinely surprised. "A painter."

"I'm Claude," he said, kissing her hand. "You're not from around here."

"No, I'm not. Who's that naked woman sleeping?"

"Well, aren't we blunt," he said, not betraying even a hint of a blush. "Just a model. See that one in the corner, with the red and blues?"

She squinted a little too dramatically at the painting. "That's a painting of a person?"

"Ouch," he said, but they both were laughing.

"You have to be closer, I guess, to see her there," he said.

She unsuccessfully tried to hold back a laugh.

"You don't believe me? Come down and look."

"But," she said sarcastically, "you might be dangerous." He met her with a skeptical glance and a smirk. "Am I going to have to cover one eye and jump on one leg to see it correctly, too?"

He took her arm, and she eyed his annoyance. He was possibly the first person she had met here who challenged her, spat everything back at her with a force equal to her own. They made their way to his studio, where he explained the painting to her.

As he began to wake up, the urge to paint engulfed him. Rebecca sat on the floor with the naked woman, nameless and completely fine with her nakedness. Drinking coffee together, the women sat quietly speaking, fascinated with one another. Claude forgot they were even there.

Rebecca, in the middle of conversation, out of the corner of her eye, saw the image in the painting he had explained to her. Of course, there it was. Right there, in plain view. She didn't understand how she didn't see it before, the red woman.

* * * * *

The painting was long forgotten on the ride into town. It still sat in Divina's bedroom. It had come to her in dream, quickly and with such sense. Why hadn't she thought of it before?

The ride to town was long, but Divina knew exactly where she was going. It was early when she left; the moon was full and night dark. The store opened early. She was there when the doors were unlocked. This was the store where John took her brothers when they needed a suit for the funeral. The place wasn't ritzy. It was second hand, in fact, but perhaps whatever drew her there in the first place was waiting for her to enter.

The radiant fabric stood out, put away in the wrong place between a ragged flannel shirt and a shelf with muddy cowboy boots. For the first time maybe ever, Divina didn't even try the dress on. It was the first thing she saw when her foot hit the tiled floor. She knew. It was perfect. The feeling was growing, swelling inside her. All of this was meant to be.

She paid the small sum and walked out onto the street into the new warm rays hitting the tar. With newfound confidence, she began her day of errands, the biggest of which had already been completed.

She returned to the farm early afternoon. Belinda cooed at the dress. Divina put it on and went to Mary's bedside to show her. The woman's eyes filled up, and fearing that she was in pain, Divina crunched low near Mary with panic etched across her face. "You look so beautiful," Mary said, her voice scratchy and coarse from not being used.

The dress was thin, a good thickness for the end of summer. It flared out on the bottom, tightened in the middle, and showed her sloping neck with a v shaped neckline.

Edgar caught a glimpse of his sister, and up until this moment, had not believed she was actually getting married. He kept waiting for someone to say it was all a joke or even a dream he had. When he saw her, he knew for sure. She would be a wife soon. It wasn't just the dress; it was the expression in her eyes, the settled woman he had never seen before.

Divina changed out of the dress rather quickly, frightened that one wrong move and she may tear it on something, or Claude would spill something on it. She placed it in the far reaches of her deepest closet to keep there until the day when she would marry John.

A knock on the door came as Divina was heading outside. "They're here," Edgar said to her as he climbed off a kitchen chair. They had been waiting for some of John's employees to come over on this, their day off. Divina had bought flowers, hundreds of flowers that needed to be planted.

They had decided instead of in a church, the wedding would be on the farm. It just needed a little work. They knew with a lot of pairs of hands, the job would be something possible to accomplish. That was something Divina had never been able to say before. A inner light spun from her eyes as she opened the door and came face to face with all the people who were there to help.

Within the hour, the plan was plotted out. Everyone was on their hands and knees, elbow deep in dirt and sweat and work. She had never seen so many flowers in one place at the same time. Beginning another row, she looked up at the person working closest to her.

Marc had been watching her for a few minutes before she noticed him. He was glad. She seemed joyful. Maybe he had come to conclusions in his own head that were completely untrue. A curious look appeared in her laughing eyes. "Yes," he asked her.

"Well, I was wondering... Is it rude to ask you where you're from?"

"It's the hair. Gives away my secret every time," he said jokingly.

They worked side by side, movements balanced together almost like dancing. The air was light, and even the humidity was not heavy that day. She gave him that prodding look again.

"You can ask me things. I don't mind," he reassured her. "I'm Puerto Rican. But I consider New York City to be where I live."

"Well, you don't have a very thick accent, but it is definitely there just below your perfect English, " she spat out.

"My parents were born in Puerto Rico. You're very intuitive. Right after I was born, we moved to the States."

"Can I ask one more?" He smiled and nodded. She could ask as many as she liked as amiable as she was. "I'm warning you. It's an odd one," she said, almost nervously.

"I am not easily offended," he stated kindly.

She peered at his hands. "It's gone now, but I swear, the tips of your fingernails were burnt when I met you."

Chapter 6

Within the first two weeks that Rebecca had been spending time with Claude, he had at least six different nude women walking around his apartment like it was the most natural thing in the world. He considered her an artist herself, so he had no second thought about it. She did have a great eye. His paintings were often void of recognizable subject matter. He'd put a circle on the canvas and expect Rebecca to see a tree with a naked woman sitting on a swing. Drawing buildings is precise, size and shape making and breaking everything. He watched her, learned. It wasn't long before what he wanted the viewer to see in his work, they saw.

Although he offered, in the beginning, he didn't think he was teaching her anything. He offered to show her how to paint, use color for emotion, release creativity from within. Rebecca didn't have the passion for sketching, so she didn't have the need to learn to paint. Instead, she got something better. She watched him. She had never seen such passion.

Only later in life would she have it for herself, after the years of searching. She had found it in her children, her family.

Claude lived as if he may not be able to keep a heartbeat if he had to stop painting even if only for a night. His whole body swayed, his eyes gave every thought and emotion away. She told him once if a man ever touched a woman the way that he smeared a color with his finger, with that careful concentration beyond known human capability, the world would never be the same.

One night, tired from school, she said her visit would be short. Often, she slept in his bed, not with him, never with him, at night. He was awake at night, asleep in day.

"Stay," he asked her.

"I shouldn't--" she began.

"I have something to give you. Just a little while."

She knew him well enough by then to know "a little while" would turn into hours of conversation. Then, again, she would fall asleep in his bed while he painted until the dawn.

"I am going to ask you something. You don't have to answer, but I am going to ask," he said, sucking the light airiness from the room and bringing in a serious setting.

She swallowed the lump in her throat. There were many questions she had been terrified of for years. Questions people just don't ask. Then again, she knew Claude, and he knew her well, and he may have the questions rattling around in that mind of his. She braced herself.

"Do you wonder why I have never asked you to model for me?"

Before she could control herself, she exhaled a loud sign of relief.

"I'm serious," he said incredulously.

"Oh, please," she said, swatting the question away as if it were the dumbest she had ever heard.

"I ask because *I* don't know why I am never going to ask you."

"I guess I am not much of a muse," she said as she let out a little laugh.

He sat next to her, brushed a strand of her golden hair behind her ears. She felt the tiny invisible hairs on the back of her neck stand straight up in recognition of his touch. Bringing her knees up and hugging them, curling herself into an odd sort of ball, she felt him put his arms around her.

It was then she realized he wasn't going any farther than that. He wasn't asking her for anything. Resting his head on her shoulder, looking at the profile of her face, he then asked the questions which once held her hostage.

"What happened to you," he asked, his voice just above a whisper, sad and prepared for the things she was unprepared to say.

It would be two years before she finally became his lover. The night when he asked her the questions, when she first cracked a hole in the dam of her walls, was the beginning night. There were no more nights in New York City when she did not sleep in his loft. She knew how much she had carved into him when, after two years, he started painting in the day and sleeping at night.

The thing he had for her which prompted her to stay was a gift. In a way, he explained, she had modeled for him, but he hadn't met her yet. She hadn't even climbed to the roof. The models did nothing for him that week. They were too far from the image he kept seeing in his mind: A red woman of fire, of blood, of love and hate. Red is strength and burning, intense grief and sweet juices. The woman in the painting is hard to see, he told Rebecca, because he painted her with complete darkness in the loft, following only the vivid form in his mind. Out of all the people he had shown it to since he met her, she had still been the only one to see the woman. You must have recognized yourself, he said to her.

In the end, she had no pictures, no paint stained tee shirts that smelled like him, no stubs of events they had gone to together. She had that painting. And if she stared just right, cocked her head as he often did when he tried to see where to place a new line, she almost swore she could see herself.

* * * * *

The event was approaching quickly like an expanding shadow or a rising moon. The flowers had taken to the soil thanks to the hours of labor, of careful handling and watering and weeding. The sun merely had to reach its home in the sky, and the flowers would come alive, reaching, rejoicing in the rays. Where dirt had been barren of green or colored fallen petals, beautiful stones from nearby rivers had been sewn into the soil, making garden paths. Nothing would be more of nature's aisle.

The planning of the wedding took longer than Divina had imagined. Details took so much time, and considering the amount of work the family decided to do themselves, it was no wonder. Belinda cooked (and cooked and cooked). Claude made the invitations out of leftover scraps he had collected from his childhood years. The little boy had crayons, wisps of tissue paper, strips of construction paper, tracing plastics, and many other small crafty objects. Armed with a paper showing how to spell everyone's name and the words he had to use, he went to work. As Divina told him, he had one of the most important jobs.

Setting a date was simple enough. John said they were getting married at this precise time on this exact day. All Divina had to do was make sure everything was ready by then.

That day had come. It had been over a month since the engagement began. The morning was cooler than usual as if the heavens were aware of their invitation and wanted the guests to be comfortable. Divina didn't have many guests. She had Belinda, a few girls from when she had studies before her parents died. John had all his employees, and his family arrived late last night. She hadn't seen them yet although they, of course, already knew Divina from when she was a child.

John's father had offered, over the phone, to walk her down the aisle.

Divina was touched but declined politely. The man let it go quickly, relieved. He had daughters himself, and they were not entirely supportive of sharing him.

Divina would be walking down the smooth stoned path in a few short hours. She would be doing it alone. Secretly, she didn't dare tell a soul what she was pretending on this day. On a late, sleepless night not long after she became engaged, she squinted her eyes closed and prayed. Her invitation floated up to the ceiling, and unsure whether anyone was listening or the words were just for her own comfort, she asked her family to her wedding. With each step she took today, her mother would be watching her fix her hair and apply her make up. Her father would arch his arm for her to take, and she would lace her hand through his guiding gesture, walking with him where he would give her away because even though, in body, he had left her long ago, she had been his all this time. She didn't dare tell anyone that the lone girl walking down the aisle didn't need to be given away because ghosts were her accompaniment.

Belinda brought her crate of make up into the bride-to-be's room. Sitting at a very old, wooden, and splintered vanity, Divina straightened her back and poised her neck to give Belinda a good aim at her face. Her eyelids were painted silver, and her lashes darkened, separated and lengthened, then darkened again. With a small brush, Belinda painted on her lips, a shiny pink, light and almost transparent. Laughing, the old woman mocked how Divina didn't need to apply blush. She had the warmth in her face already. A light dusting of powder finished off her face. At Belinda's prodding, Divina inspected herself in the mirror.

The reflection was pristine, jarring. Looking in the mirror, it was as if for a brief glance, she was seeing a stranger, as if she was seeing herself for the first time, or seeing something in herself she had never seen before. The arms and legs attached to her were no longer disproportional as they were in teenage years. She had grown into them.

Where was the little girl with no front teeth? The one who usually had a weed or two embedded in the tangles in her hair? Yes, her twenty years had been long. She was old now, no longer caught in what she thought a few months ago, that twenty years was still on the edge of a child. In fact, she thought she must have been dragging out childhood beyond, years beyond, reality. The thought even crossed her mind that maybe she should have married earlier.

Dark hair was swept up and showed her facial outline, the slight way her nose turned up at the end, the way her eyes were set in deep below her brow bone. She stared at her hands, especially the left hand with the glittery ring. Fingers she had found so thick and pudgy now had expanded, lengthened, stretched. They were long, almost reminiscent of a musician's graceful hands. They were old now, soft still in her remaining youth, but light scars scattered across them. Scars so old she had forgotten where she had received them, surely a sign that the little girl had grown up.

The dress made her more beautiful now somehow than the first time she had put it on. Maybe it was the way her hair softly swung up into a twist with the few strands, which floated down and framed her shoulders and cheekbones. Maybe it was the angelic porcelain quality of the skin on her face, covered in make up with the consistency of silk. Or maybe it was the calm and peace written on her face, on the balls of her feet, within the indents of the knuckles on her fingers.

"Oh, Child," Belinda said quietly, staring at her intently. Then, catching herself, she said, "I can't really call you a child anymore now, can I?" Divina stood up and wrapped her arms tightly around her aunt. She could hear the music.

* * * * *

The parts that drew Rebecca into Claude's life were the same that ultimately broke them apart. She finished school and began working. She went home often to France. Ever changing and excelling, she kept one foot in front of the other, always on the move.

This many years later, Claude still lived in the loft.

He painted her once. It was while she was sitting cross-legged on the floor and leaning back onto two paintings that were propped up against the wall. One was black with a few dots on the corner, and the other was an explosion like fireworks, quick brush strokes of blood red, golden yellow, forest green, and electric blue. Both pieces claimed a spot over a respectable shoulder. Unlike the other models that continued to weave in and out of the loft, she was conservatively clothed.

"Fascinating," he said to himself as his gaze rested on the scene for a moment.

"What is?"

"Your shoulder. The black painting behind you looks like it has the consistency of water because your shoulder seems to be going through it. Amazing."

"Is this the part where you tell me this is a painting waiting to happen, and all I need to do is strip off all my clothing?"

"No, I promised you. I can't ask you anyway. I don't know why," he said, his voice coarse and dusty.

A watercolor painting the size of a desktop was drying on the floor near her. It looked like fire smearing into a gray smoke or gray clouds. Because it was still wet, the paper was almost like fabric, bending and forming. She wrapped it around her upper body under her arms, covering her shirt, tucking in the fabric that peaked out.

She looked at him expectantly.

"I can't," he said although he tipped his head and took in all the different angles.

"Paint me."

"I'm sorry--" he started to speak.

"You can find and paint beauty in a hundred naked women, but you don't want to paint me. And I am clothed. A hundred naked women who you barely speak to and don't even know."

"Exactly, women I don't care about."

"My Lover. She Who's Shoulder Is Mine. Angel of Night," she said naming off titles of works he had done.

Works of women he had cared for and painted and told her about.

"I don't think I can do it, all right? I am sorry. I can't."

"Why not," she asked harshly. Was there some part of her that he found so disdainful that he couldn't bring himself to paint it? She was beginning to feel defensive. Sure, she was good enough for the rest of it, but painting, no.

"Because... I don't know if it will look like you. If I painted you, I would want to capture it," he mumbled. In his last exhale his confidence had left with the air.

"Capture what?"

"I could paint your golden highlights, and the shadow under your chin and where your neck meets your shoulder line. But it is the rest of it. When I look at you, your beauty is something I can never paint."

"Should I be offended or flattered?"

"It's the way your lips curl when you shake a little because whatever you're feeling at the time is so much that your body is even responding. It's how you open your eyes wide enough to seem innocent and young, yet old inside."

"You've lost your mind," she said, opening her eyes a little wider just as he knew she would.

"There! See! You just did it!"

"Did what," she asked, completely confused.

"I don't want to paint your face or your skin. I want to paint the glow they have... I want to paint your spirit," he said, understanding the words only at the time when they left his mouth.

"Fine," she said while rolling her eyes slightly. "We'll stick with what you can do. Paint my youth before it is gone for good. Nothing more, nothing less."

He let out a small laugh, which made his shoulders move, the air getting caught in his chest before he could let it out. Shaking his head, he humored her. Taking a brush and a clean canvas, he walked the few steps to where she stood. With gruff hands, he pushed her shoulders back until one touched the black canvas, and then he forced the other shoulder closer to him. Then, he put one hand on her stomach to keep it still while he shoved the base of her neck with his other hand. People run into each other accidentally with more care.

Without a word, he walked away and began to paint. She was surprised at the odd and distant stare in his eyes. The man who she could feel watching her as she slept was impossible to look at now. Within a few moments, she knew she looked shaken, possibly shaken more than he had ever seen her. The warmth flooded through her body then, like a river clear and cool, expanding to every part of the cell of her being. There it was, that feeling she got when he looked at her from under sleepy eyes. The way she felt when she leaned over and let her head go limp on his left shoulder.

She stared at him. When he looked up at her again, she could tell she had done something. With all her might, she hoped she hadn't moved. She didn't want him to walk over and touch her again until after this was all over.

Her eyes narrowed sharply as he stood up. Crouching down close to her, he took a long look. A look as if he was no longer trying to find the right line or shadow.

"You're not exactly the same as the other models, are you," he said, stating it like it wasn't a question.

"Not unless you sleep with all your models..."

She was waiting for him to move her, force her muscles to bend before they could even prepare for movement. Without warning, he leaned in and kissed her lips gently. The small kiss lingered on, and although it was not defined in the world of passionate kisses, it was electric.

He then went back to his canvas without jerking her body into another position.

And when he glanced at her now, he looked at her the way he had before he began painting. He wasn't looking at the arch of her nose or the slight curl in her hair. He was looking at her.

Long after she was gone, it was his favorite painting.

Chapter 7

The wedding song was playing loud and clear from the hidden music deck. John stood, his dull brown hair combed and clean. Right now, he was the center of attention, waiting for Divina to come into sight for all to see. His tux was black, slick. Rented.

He wanted this so badly to be over. Never had he felt such fear. Please, God, if You are listening, please let this be true. His legs were shaking to such a degree that he was surprised he was still standing. Just let me hear the words. I can handle it either way.

Divina stepped out into the light. The sun uncovered her like a surprise, like a secret shining gift now exposed to the day. The guests, in rows of folding chairs borrowed from a church in town, all stood and turned, staring. Brides are beautiful naturally. Divina's loveliness was unparalleled at that moment. The little girl everyone remembered in overalls and a dirt-covered shirt was standing before them in a fist full of grace. A few loud sharp breaths were heard rumbling through the crowd.

As she began to take steps in accordance to the music, she smiled, and her eyes darted to the ground in response to their faces. She was embarrassed to be the cause of such a commotion. Her cheeks reddened. Belinda felt such pride as she thought there is that blush I was talking about.

John felt his heart drop to his knees. Despite himself, he felt he might cry. He knew instantly the truth he had been denying for years. She could break him, thoroughly destroy him, with a single look.

God, how he loved her.

Managing not to look at John her entire walk up the stone path, Divina finally reached where she was to stand. I made it without falling, she thought to herself. Half of the walk, she had closed her eyes, remembering to breathe, counting the steps she had memorized in all the practicing. Turning to face John with her eyes still closed, she took a deep breath.

John hadn't taken his eyes off of her. Slowly, her eyes opened. While it was really only a few seconds, it felt like an eternity until she met his stare.

She looked up at him, and the sweetest smile he had ever seen danced on her lips.

The ceremony began.

* * * * *

"How dare you! After all I have done for you!"

"Daddy," Rebecca began, trying desperately to break though his rage into his ears.

"We sent you away because we thought it would be good for you!"

"I know. It was good for me, but Daddy--"

"The whole point was that you were coming back," he said, exasperated.

Rebecca watched her father storm out of the room. Tears filled her eyes, but she fought them hard, fought them like it was imperative not to cry in this empty room.

She told him she wasn't coming home. New York City was full of opportunity, and she would thrive there. She was already thriving there. Pictures and awards were sent to her family in France from all of her buildings. Her buildings were in New York and not France.

Her father thought she would come back. There had been no doubt. She would come back and work here. Where was the choice in that? It was the plan. It was decided. And now, she had suddenly, out of the blue, decided to stay away? What more could there be? She had done well, yes, and he had expected it. But there was a point when she would inevitably come back home and make a career. He thought he had made this clear. No, he knew he had made this clear.

It wasn't that she said she was staying longer. She said she was staying, period.

What kind of daughter moves away from her family? He asked himself question after question. Did I not give her everything? Have I not shown her love?

"Yes, you are good parents to me--" Rebecca began.

"Obviously, not good enough," he retorted. Then, his voice turned mean, and he began to ask if she was going to come back when they got too old or sick. "Of course not," he bellowed, "because there will be something important in New York City. Some lifeless building, I suspect!"

"I met someone," she finally confided. "I have made a life there."

"The last 'someone' you met was married. What will you do when this person leaves you, too," he yelled in anger.

Shrinking back as surely as if he had struck her at that moment, she found the words to throw back at him. She remained in silence, knowing if she dared bring this to full screaming, there would be no turning back.

As he told her to take her things, she knew this was best. In a few months, she would be smiling again. Here, it may have taken years.

Her father went to work, so she had the house to herself. Even the help was nowhere to be seen. Every room she went through, she combed as if searching for the tiniest button or thread. She took only a few items. Her mother had an old quilt, and there were some books from generations ago. A dress here and a shirt there, two photo albums, and a beautiful antique clip for her sixteenth birthday from Belinda were a few other items that went in the satchel. It wasn't much, but it contained all the things she would not want to be taken away from her when the day would come. She would never beg for the things which she knew he would never give her in anger, and most of her life, she had only interacted with him in anger.

Although in the years to come, she would move to France on and off again, and live at home or nearby, she never brought the satchel back into that house. She never mentioned it. Inside, she knew he would tell her to bring it back, keep it here for safety, where he himself would watch over it. What he would never understand is that she took it all away because in the end, she knew he would take it away from her in front of her very eyes just to see the pain on her face.

Claude was the one person she trusted to take care of it for her. When she finally moved out on her own, away from New York City for the last time, she came to claim it. She took *The Red Woman* with her and some other things for her new house. There was more than she had remembered. She'd come back for the rest when she ventured back into the city. But she hadn't come back until now. Honestly, there were times when she forgot about it. She could even think of Claude, remember him and their time together, and the satchel would not even enter her mind. Then, her father died, and it hit her with a vengeance.

Burying her father was not going to be the last or even the hardest trip she would have to make, and she knew it the instant she heard the news.

* * * * *

The preacher, a young man in his late thirties, had thick mahogany colored hair and wore wire rim glasses. His voice was strong, and no matter what words he could say, the mere sound of him carried an unearthly comfort. Smiling at the couple and the guests, he made the ceremony seem to flow as if time were passing at rapid speeds.

Everyone was surprised how far he had come when he asked the question.

"Do you," he began confidently and with the rhythm of a song.

No one had any confusion when it came to John. He had loved her since she was waist high and naming frogs. So, when it came to Divina to answer the question, even John looked as if he wasn't sure what she was going to say. This was the girl who said what she thought no matter where she was or who she was with, and while it was refreshing, it caused quite a shock to most who witnessed her mere presence. Her lower lip trembled as if she might cry.

God, don't leave me now, John prayed silently.

Her eyes set on John so still. She wasn't aware everyone was watching anymore. Her mouth opened slightly, drawing in the fresh air and cooling her tongue. Her words were perfectly even, timed, strong and never wavering.

"I do," she said.

Trying to hide it, she wiped a tear away.

When she looked up again at John, she giggled. It was the first time she had ever "giggled" the kind of giggle meant only for the person she adored.

He was crying, too.

Chapter 8

The phone rang without the preparation, without the warning. No, it wasn't a bill collector. Nor was it a salesperson as his most recent model had told him. The voice that traveled to his ears was one belonging to his past, to the object of so many sleepless days.

The woman he had tried and tried again to forget about was always evident. Then, upon finding he would never forget, he tried to just put her behind him. Nothing worked. She appeared in swirls, in blank canvases. She was the blond disappearing into closing doors on the subway. She was the pale-faced girl he saw in a blur riding in the back of a taxi. No matter where he was or what he was doing, he saw her around him as if she had never left at all.

Claude knew she would come back someday. But he never expected that an unsuspecting day would end up being someday. Now, she was here, back to reclaim the old things she left with him while they were together. As he thought the many years would heal the torn wounds, he found the second he heard her voice again the battle scars opened up and flowed as fresh as the moment they were cast.

The scenes from that last day were permanently etched in his mind, in his most vivid memories. The words could run through his head with the precision of a tape, which he played over and over. And there was such truth. What drives people together often ultimately drives them apart

Continuously.

"Come with me," she said joyfully on that last day. She wrapped her arms around his shoulders as she was behind him and put her cheek against the back of his neck. Closing her eyes briefly and without his knowledge, she breathed in the scent of his blond hair.

"You know I can't," he replied. Her shoulders tightened. He had to paint. In all their time together, he never mentioned getting away, being alone together somewhere other than the loft. And while her address was the same as his, the loft was never hers. It belonged to him and always would.

On this day, she had felt one too many times the feeling of being a guest in this place, which should have been her home.

Then, before she could think or monitor her thoughts from her words, she began the discussion that she promised herself she would never bring up. Even as the first sentence came out, she knew. Inside, she dreaded it and hoped maybe she was wrong, but she knew.

"We can't stay here forever," she barked, extending her arm as a gesture sweeping over the room as if it was barely sanitary.

"This is my home," he said as his eyes narrowed, hurt but angry all the same.

She bit hard on the hook. "Your home, oh, I see. And where is my home? Tell me that!"

"Here. Here, of course, here. I didn't mean," he said, exasperated.

"Is this as far as it is going to go? Am I just going to be a woman who almost lives with you? A woman good enough to stay hidden in this apartment but not enough to be introduced to friends or family?"

"You know that is not true," he growled.

"How long have I been here with you?"

He knew somehow this question's answer had a deep impact, but he wasn't sure what she was getting at. "Years," he told her, waiting to see where this was going.

"Years." She was a silent for a moment. He shifted uncomfortably. He wondered what she suddenly wanted from him. A few moments ago, she had been perfectly content.

She had known for a long time that between the lines and within the words never said, she wanted the things that he would never give her. "I want a house," she began, almost more to herself than to him.

"This is about a building," he asked her as if she had lost her mind.

Her far off, piercing stare stopped his voice. "And I want a family. Babies." His mouth gaped. In conversations deep into night before drifting into sleep, he had spoken of the life he wanted to lead. She had said nothing when she learned, over and over again, he didn't want children. "I want a husband. Someone who will love me forever," she said wistfully, sadly.

All this time, she had been telling herself she didn't need these things.

"You have me. You're my soul mate," he said, trying to comfort her.

This she knew already, and it was the reason she had been telling herself she didn't need the other things she wanted in her life. She ran an index finger over his forehead and traced his eye lids which closed at her touch.

All the things he loved about her were the things that he didn't want. He loved the way she wanted so much out of life, to see and do everything, to accomplish what others told her she couldn't do. And there was the way he had seen her reach out and touch with hands made not of skin but of kindness, the way she scooped up a crying child who had fallen in their path or the way she treated strangers. Her heart was so big and wasn't satisfied in this small room.

She loved him deeply. She loved his passion, a passion she often lived for. Watching him paint became one of the most cherished parts of her life. He would never hurt her, never. She loved being his muse. He was strong and kind with a soft voice and even softer ear. He understood her.

"I have to go," she said, her voice betraying her. This was the first time she realized this truth.

"Yes, that is probably good. Take a walk or something," he said.

She smiled without happiness. "No, I have to go."

He knew then she was leaving him. "Don't you love me," he asked, his voice rising so high it nearly squeaked. It hurt beyond words.

She took the palm of her hand and placed it on the back of his head, drawing their foreheads to touch. "Yes, I love you."

They both knew it was over. As she left, she wondered if she was capable of love. Love was this gift from God, he told her. You fight for it. You mend, you cry, you scream, you compromise, he told her. Then, you forgive. You move on.

Ashamed and empty, she left. She knew all these things, had heard them, read them in books, saw them in great romantic movies. Inside, she felt as if she were broken a hundred different ways, and she couldn't understand how she just let go. What kind of terrible person does this to someone, she wondered. Why couldn't I just be happy? I should have been happy. I just dove in like I wanted this and then decided one day I didn't? Trying to walk without stumbling down the sidewalk, she looked at the sky.

There was a lingering feeling no one would ever love her again. Not the way he had. Before she got out of the door, he begged her to stay, wait just a while longer.

"You just sprung this on me all at once," he said. "I have to warm to the idea. I'll do whatever it takes." Looking at him, at his declaration that he would do anything, she felt even worse.

He would change it all if she let him, but she would change nothing for him. Her heart screamed to stay, let him, but she knew in her head it wasn't fair to him, or to her. Or to a family he never wanted. She could never force him to have children or marry her or move into a place with a lawn and a barbecue and a white picket fence. He was a painter. She loved him as he was. She didn't want him to change, but she wasn't the person meant to stay with him. The clashing pieces just didn't form together anymore, they cut and shattered and left gaping holes in what used to blend into one completed piece.

With that, she left him and most of her things. She left the loft and the city, her job and all that was hers for so long. Because even all she had, as amazing as it was, and as fulfilling and wonderful, it would always be just that. It would never grow or change.

And she wasn't done living, deciding. She wasn't ready for this to be it: her entire life.

She wanted more.

And she hated herself for it.

* * * * *

The ceremony was over, and it was a success. The groom's cheeks were flushed with warmth as he spoke with the guests, and Divina had a smile that never left her face.

Belinda stood near Divina during the entire reception, always less than an arm's length away. In her mind, Divina was her little girl.

The flowers were beautiful, and the air swelled with their perfume. A breeze was evident during the entire day, enough to cool the air but not enough to blow off hats or mess up hair or make paper plates float away. The sky was cloudless, magnificent. John swore it matched the color of Divina's eyes.

"You look worn out," John said to Divina as the last guest left.

Although her skin was beautiful and glowing, Divina's eye lids were beginning to droop. She hadn't realized until it was over just how traumatic it had been. The ceremony and planning and people had taken more out of her than she realized. When John noticed this, Divina almost burst out with glee. Maybe he was beginning to notice the things about her, recognize how to define the things she was almost certain no one had noticed about her before.

With one swoop of his arms, he lifted her up off the ground, one arm under her knees and the other under her upper back. She kicked her legs and laughed. Leaning her head against a strong shoulder, she yawned accidentally. Belinda watched from nearby with a twinkle in her eye.

"That's my cue," John announced, referring to the yawn. "Time to go home." With that, he began the walk back to his house, carrying Divina the whole way.

When the house became visible, Divina felt a shiver going through her. With all her attention going towards the events earlier in the day, she had almost forgotten the looming shadow of the night. Of what, she was sure, waited in the night.

Although nice, kissing John in the wedding had been awkward and downright frightening. She didn't even want to imagine... Feigning sleep, she measured her deep breaths as John carried her into the house.

He was deathly quiet, unwilling to disturb her. She felt herself being dropped, no, lowered, onto his bed. She knew this because she knew his house well. He had brought her inside the front door, taken her down a hall and turned into a room on the left side.

Then, he left the room. She peeked out of one eye, heard his footsteps coming back in the room, and snapped her lid shut again. She heard him rustling around for a while. Breathe, she reminded herself. Be confident. It's all right. People do this all the time.

When he finally stopped movement and noise, she felt his weight on the bed beside her. He relaxed, flattened out on his back. The room was dark, and he pulled a blanket from the foot of the bed up over the both of them. Then, he reclined again and didn't move.

She peeked. John had changed into boxers and a tee shirt. His eyes were closed, and he was in the lightest part of sleep. He hadn't put a finger on her. She was still in her wedding dress. Feeling a vast amount of relief and faith in him, she, as if still in sleep, moved vaguely closer to him. Her head rested near his shoulder, her foot just brushing his foot. She felt him stir, reach his arm under and around her, and then he was deep in dream.

That first night, they slept, he with his arm around her, and she in her wedding dress.

* * * * *

Rebecca had not been prepared for the life she had taken on. Upon leaving Claude and New York, she found herself doing sketches in late hours and traveling the world. She had a pleasant visit with her family in France. They wanted her to stay longer, move back in even, but she knew it would be better to leave on good terms after a short visit than leave on bad terms after a drawn out visit.

Hotels, apartments, and even a rented house here and there were temporary places to sleep, to eat, to work. None of these places begged her to stay, ingrained their imprint in her soul. It didn't take long for the loneliness to find her.

She would be sitting sketching in her note pad or perhaps leafing through a magazine. The quiet was disruptive, and although the place held no former memories of voices or images, she felt the void. The noise of pipes, nearby lawnmowers, or passing cars was deafening. Many places she stayed were in towns she had never seen, full of people she had never met. Locked inside, sketching, running around to business meetings, she found little time for socializing. Not that she had the heart for it anyway.

Although she missed Claude, it was not that she regretted her decision. The world now was different to her without him. Her skin was cold, and when she walked outside, and the wind hit her just so, her entire body felt it. In the grocery store, when a stranger would accidentally brush against her in passing or lay a hand on her shoulder to move in front of her, she would be acutely aware of the human touch. There was no room to walk through in her house where someone would lovingly scrape the palm of their hand against her back. She was truly alone. She realized she was unaware, not necessarily happier, but indifferent to what this was like before she had met Claude. This was her first chance to miss something that she hadn't even know existed.

Rebecca called her friends and family often, and during one especially strained conversation, her friend, Blanche, decided on the spot it was time to come for a visit.

When Blanche arrived, the first thing on her mind was to get Rebecca out of wherever she was staying, get her out of the rooms with four walls and windows which held closed curtains. Her friend needed to laugh again, needed to breathe the fresh air.

Within the first week, the two were regulars on the night scene. From that visit on, whenever Rebecca moved to yet another location, Blanche would come down and help her get settled.

No longer the wide-eyed girl who knew nothing of heartache, Rebecca built a wall of hopelessness and concrete around the places inside that Claude had opened in her. She was hardened. She was also ruthless. Men came and went with a vengeance, in and out of her life like Claude's models in his loft. Indifferent most of the time, she did nothing for revenge or out of anger. Mostly, she liked to hear another person's breathing in the other room, another person's footsteps. She liked having a number to call when she wanted company. But there was no real emotion attached to any of them. Some of the men she met were friends, some were honest and sweet and in love, and others were using her as much as she used them.

Although she now had a hand to hold and an arm to steady her, a voice to build her up (and, at times, tear her down), no one filled the void where Claude had been. No one knew her, at least not any more than she let them.

This cycle continued. She met a man, fancied him, listened to him speak or sing or scream. In return, she got the presence of a living, breathing, warm human being. She gave up on the notion of love again. I had my one great love of a lifetime, she thought to herself. Some people don't even get that. I should be grateful. But there is such an ache. Before Claude, she remembered always wishing, dreaming. All she had wanted was someone to care. And what did she do when she found someone to care? She left him. The guilt corroded her fairy tale hopes. In her mind, she had asked and received. Then, she had changed her mind. She felt she had no right to be asking again.

At the breaking point, Rebecca grew tired of hating herself. So tired, in fact, that she found a monster in the mirror whenever she glimpsed her reflection. Claude was in her thoughts every day. He was the last thought she had before she drifted off to sleep and the first thought even before her eyes opened in the mornings. Yet, she never considered going back. The reasons were still there. Even with nothing, she needed more than what waited for her with him. One late night, in the heat of an argument, a lean and tall man she had been seeing for a month slapped her. She, in turn, felt the ferocious pride she had been lacking for so long. When did it come this far? No person had the right to treat another this way, and she had believed this inside for years. Somehow, she had taken down the lines and rules that applied to all people from herself.

Even the comfort of a familiar voice or a whistle from the garage made her cringe. It was time to be alone. She had been alone for a while, but now she had to make it complete.

The day she left the last of her men was the day she began to glow again.

Rebecca drew more, cried less. She taught a few classes and made a few female acquaintances that had shown her kindness. It felt good to hear greetings upon walking into her buildings. Her edge was worn down, and her tongue, although always polite, was now laced with honey sweetness. People liked to listen to her speak, liked to be around her. She didn't walk like a scarred animal anymore, no more clinging onto an arm. Holding her neck straight, eyes level, and head up, she found herself smiling even at the smallest sights.

She found she liked herself again by being alone.

Chapter 9

The sun rose early at John's, showing its face through the crack in the curtains.

Unsure at first where she was, Divina's eyes popped open in a burst of energy. John was still close although she had wiggled out of his grip. He faced away from her, but she recognized his outline. It was quite possibly the closest she had ever been to John and noticed him as he was now and not remembering him as a ten-year-old child. Living so long in this room, John was accustomed to the early light. Obviously, it didn't even wake him anymore.

Although warm and safe, Divina felt the deep need to get up away from their sleeping positions. Quiet as a mouse, she tiptoed barefoot on the floor, careful when she rose off the mattress not to send creaks and squeaks to John's ears.

The house was theirs alone for now. Belinda was staying with Claude and Edgar and Mary, all of which would inevitably move into John's house or buildings on his property in a few days. They wanted the couple to be alone together first; it was customary. Even the cook and other nearby workers had been given the next few days off.

Divina walked down the hall, and no matter how far she got, she calculated every step to be silent. What on earth could I be doing up this early, she wondered. Then, it came to her.

"Of course," she whispered with great relief.

Even she couldn't believe she hadn't thought of it earlier. It was so simple. The cook was off, it was early morning, and breakfast needed to be made. Her stomach was tipsy, unsure, and braided with nerves. The whole event seemed bizarre as if at any moment she would wake in her own bed with Claude down the hall and Edgar sneaking out before the dawn. But John would be hungry. She was sure he wasn't feeling the least bit apprehensive. It was morning, a morning that was a world away from the last.

She was a wife now and he a husband.

She succeeded in preparing a large breakfast without making too much commotion. Scrambled eggs that reflected her nerves came out just a little runny. The smell filtered into John's room. It was heavenly. He awoke slowly, long before he opened his eyes. He reached over and felt the empty indent. With a start, he sat up, and his eyes popped open. Then, the smell from her cooking hit him like a fist. He let out a breath, which he hadn't even realized he had been holding in.

He ventured towards the kitchen and stopped in the doorway. Flour from rolls dotted her cheek and the back of her hands, and she swayed back and forth, stirring a glass of freshly squeezed orange juice. Her lips were pursed together, and she was humming.

She was dancing as she cooked. He cleared the air with a cough to announce his presence. When she jumped, startled, and turned to look at him, she saw he looked at her with such admiration. It was then that the smell of her breakfast entered her nostrils, too, and she felt hungry. The butterflies were gone.

"How long have you been up," John asked her, still a little surprised at all the work she had done in the kitchen.

"A while," she answered, then continued to hum and sway without thinking.

"You know you didn't have to do this," he said, waiting for an answer.

"I wasn't going to wait for you to make me breakfast."

"Oh, I see," he said, taking his first few steps into the kitchen.

Divina turned her back to him and rinsed out a dish in the sink. Her gaze lingered out the window nearby. John walked up behind her, curious to see what she was so engrossed in outside.

"What is it," he asked while squinting his eyes and looking out the window. He didn't see anything that fascinating.

"That pink," she said.

"What are you talking about," he asked, practically pushing his face to the glass of the window.

He was very close to her now, and she waited a long time before deciding to move. Natural, she told herself. It took her a few expanded seconds to command her arm to gently rest on his back.

"There, the sunrise. That pink between the horizon and the white light you shouldn't look at. I've never seen such a pink," she said. He just nodded although she could tell he had no idea what she was talking about.

With her small gesture of touch from her arm, he gathered a green light. Before she could react, he grabbed her around the waist and kissed the tip of her nose. Then, as a gentleman and as a safety measurement, he took a step back and peered into her eyes. He wanted to see her reaction.

Obviously, surprise shook her a bit, but it calmed her fear sweetly.

Shaking her head, she took another step back from him. "Sit," she said, motioning to the table. "I didn't cook all this for nuttin'."

"Whatever you say," he replied, and she was unsure whether he meant he'd eat the food or whether the comment had a grander scope than that.

Eyeing his place at the head of the table, her mind instantly wondered whether to sit on the opposite end, across from him, or right next to him. Gathering her courage, she pondered the situation. While small, she knew it held more weight than most would believe. A lady of the house would sit on the opposite end, across from him, because then she would have the same ranking as he did, and she could discuss things straight on without turning her head. A loving, loyal wife, on the other hand, would sit next to him, close to quickly fetch his plate or touch his arm when he said something humorous. She knew he would want her to sit next to him. If not today, there would be a battle in the immediate future if she took the seat opposite of him. His eyebrows would rise today, but he may wait before saying anything about the matter until another time.

As she sat next to him as if it were the most natural thing in the world for her to do, she smiled at him, and he returned her kind look. Best let him think he has won one, she thought. This one doesn't matter. The others will not be so easily won.

"Why do you look so happy all of a sudden," he asked when he noticed her mischievous expression.

She stretched her neck and bent her legs to lift her just high enough off the chair to plant a kiss on his cheek with rapid speed. "Drink your orange juice, Husband," she said.

"Yes, Wife," he replied, and when the word left his lips, it traveled up and down his spine. The word was sweeter on his mouth than even her cooking.

* * * * *

A miraculous event occurred in Rebecca. She found she could be alone and not be lonely. Despite whether she found grocery shopping exhilarating because of comfort from accidental human closeness, when she went home, she liked the silence. There was no need for her to speak. No one was there to bark commands, to drag her down with weapon words.

There was no one to offend or hurt. Although painful, it had been easier than she thought it would. Long walks and late nights with even later mornings colored her schedule. She took up cooking and gave out dishes to her neighbors and those who she referred to as "acquaintance friends."

Alone in the house with music playing in the background, she always danced when she cooked. Sometimes, she even sang along. The blue of the sky and the warm hues of the sun were electric to her now. She figured they must have changed somehow. They had never been so bright before.

Upon a whim, she went to a furniture store and had a rocking chair made. She placed it on her back porch in the small brown house she had been renting for four months. On the outskirts of some unknown city, she could see for miles. The sky was never ending, swallowing the thinning ground. The yard was well maintained but unpretentious. A thin, blossoming tree with white flowers stood on one side while a few evergreens were approaching full size on the opposite side on the lawn. The grass was cut yet thick, and in the earliest hours deemed appropriate, when the dew was still wet and cold, it was the perfect place for a barefoot excursion. The manicured line ended abruptly and erupted into the wild fields just beyond her property. Wildflowers grew in thick bunches, free and uneven, hand planted by God. The area directly blending into the fields was forest and so deep and dark that light could not be seen between the trees. There was a precise moment in the evening, just before the sun slipped down, when a few deer would roam just beyond their hidden home in the woods.

On the mundane, repetitive evenings when birds in flight would twist in the air like kite tails, Rebecca would think each moment's beauty surpassed the last. A neighbor walked by on a last minute lazy stroll, and noticed her, and yelled out a quick comment as he passed. "Beautiful, isn't it," he asked.

She glanced at him, arms folded across her chest and hair gently flying behind her. Her face then returned to the sunset to which he was referring. "Yes, it is," she replied.

"It's a painter's sunset," he nonchalantly said before disappearing around the corner.

Before Rebecca could feel a dagger cutting open sealed memories, a fog rolled in covering the blaze of the comment. A sullen subtle smile wound tight on her lips. The light in its last visible scene was a mix of blending bleeding reds, rolling oranges, and melting white.

The crack of the screen door slamming was louder than the traffic in her ears or the bird's song. Inside, she fumbled, flipping through item after item in a chest of drawers. With it in sight, she dug deeper, flinging what was blocking the object from her reach at the bottom of the drawer. The screen door slammed again behind her as she stood outside, the last of the watercolor sky dripping with the moon on its heels, chasing it to the other side of the world.

Quickly and with precision, she snapped picture after picture until there was no film left from her new roll.

She just happened to know a painter.

* * * * *

John sat quiet, silently protesting the intrusions of employees who came to the door despite their day off. When a man with a piece of registered mail came knocking, John didn't care how cute Divina looked as she bounded up towards the door. Already he was jealous of her diverted attention.

In his private thoughts, he cursed himself for not pushing to have a honeymoon far, far away. Somewhere tropical or snowy, somewhere busy or secluded, he didn't care as long as it wasn't here. Because here was foreign despite how many times they had sat at this table together. The rules were gone now, and he had no idea what the new ones were.

John had always been the one who opened doors for her, who laughed at her jokes even when they weren't all that funny. He had been the one who watched her from afar, watched her walk into his house time after time, year after year. She never looked at the place the way he wanted her to see it. In his heart, he wondered if even after the wedding she would take each step as if a visitor, as if the neighbor from down the road. Even before he inherited the place, before he was the head of it all, he knew he wanted her there. Down the hall in the tiny bedroom where his mother painted trains on the wall, he picked out the rooms she would like when he married her. All this when he was still a boy himself. Although he may have wished it, and there was still a flutter of hope, he felt that as a girl, she never saw her future within these walls. Then again, Divina had been surprising him on a regular basis her entire life, so maybe if he found the right words to ask, then he would get the answers he wanted to hear.

Breakfast had gone well. Conversation didn't have to be forced. While their topics and words were simple in nature, they flowed effortlessly and without resistance. As nice as it was, John couldn't help wondering how the words would change on them.

When would the real connection begin? It wasn't as if between the comments on the weather they would suddenly be discussing their dreams and what kept them awake in the night. As Divina came back from another interruption, she glanced around the kitchen they still sat in. Taking it in like it was new, John watched, his gaze transformed and his mind forgetting any and all small worries that plagued him during waking hours of the day. He could practically hear the "snap" of her, of her fitting into this house.

"Maybe if we sit in the other room, people won't see us from the window. Maybe they won't feel as welcome," she offered.

"Sure, good plan. Let's hide," he said, grabbing her hand as he took to leading her towards one of the living rooms. He figured the one on the top floor, with the ceiling of skylight, with all the plants which thrived although all he ever did was water them once a day, was the one room no one would see them in from the outside of the house. Ah, yes, the one room that was theirs before childhood was unraveled from around them.

"I remember this room," she said, smiling at the sight of the approaching doorway.

"Close your eyes," he said, suddenly stopping, still holding her hand.

"That's okay, really," she replied.

"I am serious. How long has it been?"

"Years," she answered. "There was no reason to go in there. I'm twenty years old. I don't run around and scream and make up stories anymore."

"Humor me," he said, taking the hand that didn't hold hers and closing her eyelashes for her.

"Fine," she said, her word kind but serious.

She felt him guide her carefully, but she knew the way. The hall was straight; there was nothing for her to stumble on. Nevertheless, each step was slow and measured, and he led her as if she were breakable. It took much too long to reach the old room, but neither minded nor said anything. She decided not to pay it any attention. She felt him slow down, no longer supporting her steps. They had stopped completely, and he turned her, so she knew she was in the doorway, facing the room, staring straight into it.

"Open your eyes," he said.

She obeyed.

Her expression illuminated her surprise as she absorbed the room. She remembered it as a child, with toys hidden in leaves and blankets covering half the furniture in make shift forts. He had played along well although never sure of himself in her wild ideas. One day, they were in the jungles, deep in the corners of the room under the brush of tall dogwood trees with white blossoms. On the next day, they were in a massive war against poachers, on all fours, she an elephant, and despite her lack of enthusiasm, he a dog. John never understood why she rolled her eyes when all he wanted to be was a golden lab. This is where she went to play, this room the one the adults stuck the children in, never fully understanding the curious smiles or screaming laughter erupting from the mere mention of the room.

Not only was the room restored, it exceeded its previous scene. The plants were bigger, more elaborate and healthy. Divina never knew if it had been well taken care of when John was a child. It had always been just kind of there. The furniture was new, yet soft and comfortable, definitely not something put out to entertain guests. The tables were wood and hand cast iron legs covered in vines and leaves. An elaborate spring system was going as clear water trickled down an artificial patch of cement around some vegetation. The cement, which took the water on its travels around the room, was made of stones and cobble colored sand. Flowers were few and far between, but they burst out like explosions all over the room. A sharp yellow here, an electric purple swimming near one small gathering of the running water. The final touch, a live frog jumping and croaking near John's feet, made Divina clasp her mouth with both hands in obvious glee.

"Oh, John, it's wonderful," she exclaimed, nearly breathless.

"You're twenty years old," he said with mock sincerity. "Don't go off and start making up stories."

She reached out without thought and grabbed his arm. When realizing what she had done, her eyes softened just a little, not enough for him to notice. But she had felt the comfort in it, the natural way she had acted like they had been married for years. A nearby chair, forest green and overstuffed, called to her. She sat with one swift movement, never stopping her gaze from staring around her.

Just as a child who has just been given candy, John found the same rapture fascination in her reaction as she did to the room itself. Quietly, without daring to say it, he almost wanted her to stand up and command to have a few old wool blankets to start building a fort. They could be on an adventure, shipwrecked on a deserted island, hunting in the Congo. They could be warriors, animals, lost, seeking treasure. In a way, he felt silly at the thought that he couldn't remember a time they had played house like normal children. Well, they were certainly making up for it now.

The two spent the rest of the day in that room, their bare feet on the cold and dull tile floor. There were no more interruptions, no more unforeseen thieves of attention. Words ventured, polite but stabbing, a little deeper. In memory, they reminisced about the old days, the days before, as if they needed their beginning to start when and only when they voiced the past. The words themselves were not of utter importance; there were no grand announcements or promises made. Nothing pushed. But it was the rhythm of the sound of voice, the recognition of the newness, which made the uncomfortable seemingly comfortable. In all the fear of where should they go and what should they say and how should they say it, with such tiny baby steps they had began the path, which they sealed in stone yesterday. For now, at least, the stirring waters were swaying with calm.

Chapter 10

Rebecca sent the pictures to Claude every month. Pictures of skies and birds, nameless people standing in a suddenly picturesque scene, sunsets and rises, rains and snows showed up in manila envelopes. Her writing was clear despite the lack of a return address. She enclosed no letters, no explanations why the pictures were sent or where they were from. The only reason he knew they were from her was the writing of his address on the outside of the envelope. Only she swirled a pen in her hand that precise way to make the letters and numbers seem to sing her name. Never a return address because she didn't want him to know where she was, and she didn't want him to write. Most importantly, she didn't want him to tell her to stop sending the pictures.

Knowing the past is sometimes better cut off, she still couldn't do it. She didn't want to see him or hear from him. She didn't even want to know how he was doing. It felt better not knowing, but she knew he was still painting. And she hadn't left him any pieces of her. This way, they would be connected still, and it made her feel better just to know he would touch the same prints that her hands held not long ago. Strange and silly, she knew, but there was such a need. Rebecca knew sending pictures was the best way, better than showing up or phoning. This way she could stay on her own, without him, because she didn't need him. What was left was wanting him to be near and to change and to fix things that cannot be fixed. She compromised with herself, telling herself to send the pictures and maybe one day, while she was minding her own business, walking into some bank or hotel, she would see her picture made into a painting on the wall. Then, she would know he hadn't lost everything. Not even his muse.

Blanche continued her visits, the time between each one visibly decreasing. Rebecca was strong now; there was no doubt of that. In the beginning, Blanche had seen her friend, watched every movement, wondering if, and then, when her beloved friend would run home to the family which hurt her time and time again. It had been a while since Rebecca took a second glance at any man, so when Blanche suggested the vacation, a stint on the riverboats, Rebecca thought nothing of it. She thought she'd have a few days alone, show her stature, and gracefully mingle with other well to do people.

When she heard the laughter and saw the man, every pore in her body engulfed the breeze and chilled her from the outside in. There she was, minding her own business, looking over the side of the riverboat, thinking what a picture this was. She hadn't brought a camera. When she turned and saw him, even the word "picture" was erased from her mind. But it wasn't until he turned and noticed her staring at him, when their eyes met, that she knew for sure. She felt like she had been hit over the head with a baseball bat. All the things she said she didn't want, and all the times she knew she was happier now alone than when she was with someone, they vanished. Perfection is impossible, but compatibility is rare yet imaginable.

Mr. Hamilton walked over, entranced. She told him right away, partly to test him and partly to hear herself say the words. This was it. All it took was one look, one conversation, and her heart melted, kneading all the holes out and filling them. This fierce wretched intuition in her gut told her like never before that this man was her destiny. She'd known what she had wanted before, known her career would be all right, figured how her life would lead, but never like this, with this certainty. The doubt was gone. He could have been anyone, a terrible person, a woman dressed as a man, even married already. Worst of all, he could have been a painter. How could she know? She wasn't sure how she knew or why she felt so strongly, but there wasn't a glimmer inside, not even the tiniest voice which said to her, you may be wrong, and this may hurt you. Always cautious and wary, this was different. Jumping in with both feet, Rebecca never looked back, and even in her final moments, she never second-guessed herself. In all that time, never. Never.

On that first night, she could almost feel the joy of children, of stability, of a rich and prosperous life. The warmth in his clammy hands when he said "I do" seemed to foreshadow all the times ahead when he would hold her hand, make her smile, bite along with her through the most painful times in their life together.

Like a cleansing rain had drenched her, like she had bathed in a fountain of deep prophetic meaning, she was born anew that day. Rebecca had found what she had been searching for, and in completing a circle she was sure would never be finished, without realizing it, she had completed another person who had been searching for her just as long and with just as much at stake.

* * * * *

Divina and John Cordston's first few weeks of marriage were simple, shy, even bashful. Laughter came easily despite the rumble of nervousness that was sewn into it. Conversations stayed light and polite, airy and professional. After the first three days, people began to reappear. Cook came back, so Divina refused to prepare meals, which displeased John, but pleased Cook. Employees were ordered to listen to Divina if she ever asked for anything to be done. She was to have as much power as John, but to a point. Divina wasn't allowed to make big decisions without consulting John, although John was allowed to make decisions without consulting her, which she found highly offensive. She pushed it into the back of her mind. Figuring she had to prove herself, she had no doubt in her role in the future. Once she showed everyone, then she thought her status would be raised.

Arguments were silence, but silence not always meant an argument. He pursed his lips into a thin, tightened line while she usually left the room muttering about some errand she needed to get done immediately. The steam would filter out, but within them both, the heat rose. Voices above a soft hum had yet to be heard in the house.

And then there was the romance.

Or, in better terms, the fear of romance. On the third week, John finally kissed Divina good night, on the cheek. While they slept in the same room, she was afraid and unsure. He respected that, but his patience was wavering. Progression was slow but steady, with John finding ways throughout the day to touch her hand or brush back a lock of her hair.

Eventually, it happened before she even thought about it. John fell asleep one night, about a month into the marriage, and she ran to the mirror, wanting to see if she looked different. The whole mechanics of it had been strange and awkward, and she didn't understand why she had been so worried about the whole situation. That was what all the fuss was about? That would have sent her straight to hell if she had gone ahead before taking vows? As days wore on and she grew more confident, understanding, it became a more pleasant experience. Her birthday came quickly, and she found herself staring into twenty-one years of live. Yet, she still couldn't consider herself someone's wife, someone's lover. It was surreal as if she could wake up in the morning, and it all would have been a dream. A good dream, she decided, but a dream nonetheless.

"Are you awake," John whispered to her in the earliest hours.

She had grown used to the light and slept later. She stirred but didn't reply with words.

"Come on, twenty-one," he said proudly, as if she had forgotten.

"I'll be twenty-one for a whole year, John," she muttered, not fully out of sleep.

"Happy Birthday," he said before getting up, leaving her to finish resting.

She sank into the fresh indent he had left, smelled his shampoo on his pillowcase. Smiling in the recognition, her eyes fluttered open, old and sultry. In her head, she wondered if this simple smell was making her fall in love with him. She wasn't sure what love felt like or how she'd know, but she thought maybe this is what all those songs were about.

Midmorning, Divina got up and dressed and stretched her arms to the ceiling, touching the top of each doorframe she passed as she made her way to their room. Their room was the one with the skylight and plants, the one where she read books and listened to him talk about work. When he was in the house, she knew he would be there waiting for her.

"So, did you get me something good," she asked him while she sat next to him in a love seat style piece of furniture. Her eyes darted around the room noticing that there was no pretty box or gift-wrap in sight.

"You mean, being your husband isn't enough?"

She smiled sarcastically, knowing him too well to play into the game.

"I know you are bored here, Divina," John said seriously.

She jumped right in, exclaiming, "I am not!"

"You sew the same shirt over and over. And, as much as you want me to, I can't let you into the core of my business."

The curl of her lips lost their momentum. He saw her hurt and quickly went on speaking.

"I have a business proposition for you," John said.

Belinda was in the hall. She didn't mean to listen, but she didn't want to make her presence known now after she had been standing there for just a little too long. Claude was in a part of a newly remodeled building where Mary was being treated.

"Go on," Divina insisted.

"I want you to fix up the house," he stated with great pride.

"John, that is ridiculous. This house doesn't--"

"Not this house, your house and part of your land. See, the smart thing here is that where you used to have that immense garden when we were kids, that is where some of the most fertile soil is."

She swallowed and asked without belief, "Really?"

"Yeah, it would be great for both of us. I just came into some more money, so we can finally afford it. Otherwise, we would have done this long ago." John looked at her, waiting for some reaction, anything at all. Even if she hated it, she wasn't showing anything.

Belinda, still in the hall listening, had to cover her mouth to stop from yelling in glee. She knew what Divina would do before Divina did, so Belinda didn't even have to look in the room. Divina jumped as if trying to escape from her own skin and threw herself into John's arms.

"Thank you! This is so wonderful," she screamed, nearly sobbing. The excitement painted her face a rosy pink, and her eyes jumped more than John had ever seen. There was more passion in that one embrace than there had been in any given moment since they had first met as children.

John knew then that he had made the right decision and given her the perfect gift.

Belinda slipped out of the hallway before Divina could come bursting out to find her and tell her the good news. What a great day for Divina! She had a thousand ideas running through her mind, and Mary was comfortable although straining to stay around a little longer, and Claude was about to go to school and the happiest she had ever seen him. Divina felt like she was taking a walk in a fairy tale or, at least, in another person's life. All these wonderful things crushing her with the warmth of a hug, squeezing her bones and filling her insides with exuberance. Right now, if she wanted to, she could go outside, and she could fly.

She did the closest thing to flying. She took giant leaps to the door and ran outside. "Edgar," she yelled. His head peaked out from a building, and he dropped his tools, then met her running halfway. Before he could even ask, she ran her words together as if they were racing. "Birthday present--fixing up my house--making it what it was--John's gift to me--the best gift ever--think we should paint the house white again--or maybe try something new--"

It took Edgar a moment to catch it before he understood, then he threw his arms around his sister, something he hadn't done since she had gotten married. His smile was as wide as the horizon. He may live in John's basement apartment, but there were no ties to the wood, to the rooms, to any memories. Divina was talking about home.

"When can we start," asked Edgar, his voice full of more anticipation than anyone had ever heard.

John came out, following the wild ramblings of his wife. "As soon as you want," he answered. "I can spare a couple people to help you, not many, but a couple."

"I'd like to, John," Edgar said with pure professionalism.

"I assumed as much. Why don't you and your friend be the ones to assist Divina? The guy who speaks Spanish," John said, not really asking.

Edgar tried not to roll his eyes. Although young, Edgar got along well with Marc, had come to know him well. They had each other's back and had gotten one another out of more than one catastrophe. "The guy who speaks Spanish" wasn't a title Edgar appreciated, but he took it all the same. It was best not to get into a match with John.

"Marc," Edgar said, drawing out the name so that everyone heard it clearly, "is deeply involved in some work right now. When he takes a break, I'll tell him. I'm sure he'll go for it."

"Great," Divina shrieked, throwing her arms around Edgar again. Edgar, unprepared for the sudden shock of another taste of family affection, blindly returned his sister's hug. He could feel her age now. She was no longer a child raising him, and while there were days when he felt so small and young, usually the majority of the time, he felt as old as she now looked to him. The sight of her made him proud somehow, like he wasn't sure how or when she made it, but she had come across the finish line long ago. He must have missed it, wasn't paying attention when she bounded into her own skin, her own life.

Eyes bright and hair brushed back sweeping in the quiet wind, Divina's skin glowed with radiant youth surpassed by childhood and embraced by the woman she had become. The little flame inside, the one that ribs wrap around and remains if you tear a person apart, the flame that makes a person who they are and is the essence that remains after breath is gone, was growing higher and higher in Divina. Edgar could see it. Where there had been a faint smoke smell was now a blaze of orange and red. And, upon recognizing it, Edgar realized he, too, had taken this from her. The way he walked, the strides he took, the pride and strength in his ability were all a gift from her. This was something he never knew until just then. Until just then, he didn't even know she owned such precious things. Someday, he promised himself, he would ask her about this strength, ask her if she got it from their parents as he got it from her. There were many questions from the times when he was too young to remember. For some reason, it was only now that he considered she had these answers.

"I'll go into town today," Divina stated gleefully. "We can start tomorrow!"

"But today is your birthday--" John began, upset she wanted to go somewhere today.

Her quick glance in his direction told him that she was going. There was just too much to contain until tomorrow.

"And," John finished his sentence, "you should do whatever you want."

"Thanks. Does anyone want to come along?"

Divina was practically ready to jump into the nearest vehicle and go into town.

She looked as if she might consider riding farm equipment. John felt a sting from her open invitation and shrugged it off. No one volunteered. Secretly, John was glad.

"Give me a couple minutes," John replied as he began walking quickly back to the house to get a few things.

Divina was so excited that her hands were shaking.

* * * * *

Rebecca didn't send Claude pictures, letters, or anything else after she met and married Mr. Hamilton. The contact was completely severed. At least, until after Edgar was born.

Mr. Hamilton was infatuated with his wife, something he was very proud of. She was so fascinating with wild stories and great successes. Tales of woe and splendor spilled off her tongue with as much emotion and talent as great storytellers. She fell in love with him, she believed, the very moment before she even saw him, when she heard him laugh. After that, she just kept falling deeper and deeper.

The fear remained. Rebecca was terrified that she would mess it up, become unhappy and discontent and move on. She figured it was what she did whenever she started to care. Then, Divina came along, and the deal was sealed. That baby girl was the first taste she had which made her believe in her ability to love completely and fully and infinitely. Yet, this was a child, part of her, which lived inside her and shared her heartbeat at one time. No man could ever claim that of Rebecca's heart, although there were nights, when she was close to her sleeping husband, her ear listening to the pulse as it matched her own. She would slow or quicken her breaths to make her heart beat speed up or slow down, whatever it took to match his. It was the closest she knew of their love.

They fought. They screamed. But Rebecca was addicted to when they would make up. She loved the way he listened, and she would listen, too. They were committed. Nothing could stop them, and whatever they lacked for each other in the beginning, they found in the bond with their daughter, and after another six years, their new son. Fights no longer made Rebecca think things would be over. Because, they always fought it out until they weren't mad anymore. Mr. Hamilton had taught her how to forgive, and although she thought she knew, she didn't. She not only had to forgive her husband, but she had to forgive herself for making mistakes, small and life altering. When she did that, the peace she had been searching for was found. It was in the way her husband laughed and her daughter gurgled baby nothings. Rebecca had a husband, a little girl, and baby boy who was starting to come around. She had a life, and she wasn't prepared for or expecting things to be shaken up.

Then, her father died.

She found herself in Claude's life again, not that she had been gone from his life, but that she had erased him from hers. Everything that contained them in his loft again seemed to be sucking her right back in.

Chapter 11

The dying grass was covered sporadically with unopened paint cans. Divina had gone into town and come back with a truckload of essentials. In the store, she had peered into eggshell, off white, crème, ivory, beige, and a hundred other variations.

Squinting her eyes, examining each one, trying to find the differences between the nearly identical hues, she finally picked one: White.

The old buildings on her premises held even older supplies such as a partially rusted ladder, a box of unopened paint brushes. Edgar and Marc dragged them out onto the lawn while Divina was in town with John, who patiently watched her go over every possible detail while shopping.

John had never seen her like this, with that determined glaze in her eyes. Surely, he knew she was capable, but he worried she might be overdoing it. Seeing her excitement and her need, he didn't voice a word to her about his concerns. This was her house and her past, and while he may have never heard her say it, he knew she was tied somehow. She had wanted this since she was a little girl.

The house crumbled completely after Rebecca died, but in the years before Claude's birth, anyone could see the wear on the place. The farmlands did well, but the house fell apart bit by bit. New money went to the fields, to the equipment, and eventually, to Rebecca's illness in the years before her death. There were no conversations in the house for the children to overhear, no glimpses at a deteriorating woman, but the feeling was there under the surface of the air. The paint on the outside of the house had been peeling since Divina had her first memory. The statues and artwork were barely visible by cascading plants. No one had the time to worry about such small, trivial things. Work needed to be done, children were to be raised, and, at times, Rebecca had to be cared for. John's parents had told the children that it had been a heart condition and to watch for Claude because he might have it too, which is why the doctors gave him medication.

Divina never talked about it. She gave Claude his medication, which was prescribed. John never said a word. Belinda didn't talk about Rebecca's sickness, although she often spoke of Rebecca. The situation was there, brewing, but they never brought it up because they were too busy pushing it away.

John knew in the weeks ahead that he would be busier than he had ever been. He would be surpassing Mr. Hamilton's most prosperous year this year. John didn't want to leave his wife with nothing to do but watch him work. So, without telling her the reasons, he gave her this project. He thought nothing much of it. It would keep her happy and busy. The price wasn't terrible because she would be doing all of the labor with Edgar and Marc, both wonderful employees, but easily replaced. John had hired many new employees since marrying Divina. Time was going quickly. Sooner than later it would be their second anniversary.

Evening came quickly, and morning appeared in almost moments. Divina felt the surge of energy, the mold of pride. She was about to make everything bright again. Her attention needed to be diverted from her husband. The relationship had been going well, but he wanted children. She was surprised they had waited this long. Still unsure how she felt about that, she was at least getting used to the rituals of being married, of incorporating someone else into a life which once belonged to only her. In a lot of ways, they both emotionally remained independent, but it was the close quarters that were the hardest to get used to. John was around every corner, followed her into every room, and remained by her side as loyal and attached as one of her own limbs. Divina was glad work was going to take up some time, and now she could even go out of the house without having to make up an elaborate story. John never could understand why she just needed a walk once in a while, alone.

It was time to build on what was left of the past.

* * * * *

"You look well," Rebecca said to Claude.

"Thanks. You... It's nice to see you again," he responded, noticing the wear on her more and more.

He was surprised her father had died. A bitter, hard old man who hated him for stealing his daughter from France, Claude figured the old man would outlive him for sure just living off the amount of hate in his soul. Yet, he had died, and Rebecca was here now.

"Do you want to sit," asked Claude, pulling a wooden stool out from under a few drying paintings, propping up the paintings against a couple others against the nearest wall. He patted the seat on the make shift chair.

She sat, suddenly aware of her exhaustion. The room began to spin, and she could feel her pulse in her ears, beating a tireless song. The rip of pain shot up her spine, causing her to kneel over. It was as if her bones were expanding and her skin was thinning, stretching to accommodate them, so she wouldn't burst.

"Jesus," he muttered, grabbing her before she fell off the chair.

She held up a hand, regaining her composure although the pain lingered.

"Should I call someone," he asked. He didn't know whether he meant a doctor or a friend or a therapist.

"No, I'm fine," she finally replied, catching her breath.

His face softened and he asked her, "Does this happen often?"

Her eyes, which had been peering at the floor, rose to meet his stare. They were big and still full of life, but he saw the gray tint, the fog covering the bright white, which used to be there, which he painted in her portrait.

She didn't have to open her mouth for him to know the answer.

Her eyes left his quickly, darted and remained at her hands. She crossed her fingers and picked at a stray cuticle on her index finger. Without looking up, her shoulders sank, as if she had not wanted it this way, and she let out a little laugh.

"I have a family now," she said. Her eyes welling up, but she kept them back, kept back the trembling in her legs that would not be still.

"That's great," he said although with sympathy.

"My husband is wonderful. And my children, my children…" she drifted off. The flood inside her joined the flesh and blood. The serene acceptance blanketed her. Yet, the grief was eternal. Her work would never be done; her children had so much need left in them.

"How bad is it," Claude asked, gently pushing her to find the answer.

"I'm sick," she said simply, and it was as if she had never said it out loud before. Her head lowered even more; she still hadn't looked at him. The tears were gone now, pushed back to where no one could reach them.

"Does your family know?"

Claude knew it was probably impossible for her to hide it from them, but he also knew she had a way of springing things on people when they least expected it, things that had been obvious but unseen.

"I'm getting better," she said quickly, more as if she was trying to convince herself than him. He gave her a look that said she hadn't answered the question. "They know I'm sick, but they don't really understand... They've been great, and I've been getting the best treatment possible, but..."

He put his arm around her, unsure why she was here, if it was for him or for her things. He wondered what she wanted from this or if she even knew. Even through her clothes, he could feel how her bones were pressing against her skin. She seemed small now, even feeble, but he knew her well.

"There is strength inside you still, Rebecca. I know you can feel it. Listen," he said softly, her ears taking him in like a sponge with water. "Listen, I can hear it."

She closed her eyes, drew in a deep breath. Finally, she looked at him again, her eyes opening slowly and deliberately. "I can hear it," she whispered. The breath from her lungs and the warmth of her life was singing.

"You have a long way home," he said. "Are you staying?"

She honestly had thought she would walk in and walk out within minutes. This wasn't a question Rebecca had been prepared to answer. It wasn't one she wanted to think about either. Claude saw the dilemma on her face, in the shrugging of her shoulders. He wasn't going to ask again. Each moment she stayed would be one more minute he had with her, but he would always wonder if within the next she would walk out the door. Claude tried not to move too quickly, her eyes so sad and fatigued as if she couldn't keep up if he gestured with normal speed. He tried to relax, to bring down the high levels of pressure in the room, in the mere air around them.

* * * * *

Marc leaned over a can of paint, his face concentrating and stern, his hands clenching a tool as he tried to pry the can open. He was so engrossed that he didn't see Divina coming toward the house. The dawn was young, and the air still laced with chills. She was awake early and ready to begin.

"Hey," Divina greeted. His face shot towards the shattering of the silence. His widened eyes narrowed a little, and he gave her a nod in return. "Coffee," she asked him, holding out a cup.

"Thanks," he said, taking it from her. His face was genuinely pleased. Divina and Marc had barely spoken over the period of her marriage while Edgar became good friends with him. Divina, therefore, thought highly of Marc. She stayed out of most of John's business, but she knew Marc was a brilliant man. Edgar spoke well of him although John only noticed his job once in a while. Marc was quiet, but the few times he had walked in on business, she had heard him speak with such intelligence that it awed her. He only got involved when he was asked, so most of the time, he was content to work without being given much notice by anyone except the few friends he had made among the coworkers. Edgar himself had done a good job of staying away from John and Divina. Suddenly, her brother was working enough to actually earn his paycheck. The jobs were good on John's farm, the pay was fairly high when compared with the competition, and the people minded their own business while regarding everyone with a polite kindness. The close friendships were earned, and they were kept. Divina was glad Marc was there.

"Edgar's in one of the buildings," Marc said to Divina to explain her brother's absence.

She nodded in acknowledgment, then came closer to the can of paint. "Here," she said as she took the tool from Marc.

"I'll get it--" he said as she proceeded to pry the can open as if it were the simplest task she had ever completed. His eyebrows arched up a little.

"There," she said, and then she added, in case she had bruised his ego, "You loosened it for me." They both laughed a small, rumbling laugh. Divina clasped her hands together and let out a sigh. She was so ready for this.

Edgar came jogging into their realm of small conversation. Divina noticed he was taller than her now, so much taller than she ever remembered. His hands were large, scarred, and carrying some strange find from one of the buildings.

"Are you ready," Divina asked her brother, her hands on her hips showing disapproval in whatever he had spent time finding.

"Yes, Ma'am," he replied, then saluted her like she was in the military.

"Then, let's get started," Marc jumped in before they could bicker.

His words let the hot air out of the siblings, and they walked together, the three of them, towards the outside walls of the house. The old paint was so old and brittle that the majority of it wasn't even attached to the building anymore. There wasn't even a need to scrape any off.

In the back, there were two tall ladders reaching high to the roof. Edgar bounded inside the house, and up the stairs where he took out an old window at the very top of the wall, and sat on the ledge like it was a chair. Marc and Divina perched on each of the ladders, each armed with a bucket of paint. They were ready to begin. The three started with sweeping strokes, as if one touch of the brush could transform the place into a magical miracle. Three illuminating growing swatches of white began to appear on the side of the house, reaching great lengths just like the sun's rays stretching on the grass as the sun began to rise higher in the sky.

Sitting in the window with the glass out, Edgar balanced himself as if he was safer there than standing with both feet on the ground. It wasn't long before he began to swing his legs with the momentum of his thoughts.

"Hey, Divina," Edgar said to his sister, who along with Marc, was fairly close to him.

"Yeah," she asked.

"Do you remember the time Claude was-"

"Edgar, I really don't think Marc wants to hear family stories the entire time we work on the house," Divina interrupted. Also, she knew eventually the memories Edgar would speak of would be too personal, would be of things even John didn't know about.

Edgar laughed out loud. "He's never minded before," Edgar said.

Divina was surprised. Sure, they were friends, but her brother had a habit of keeping things in, especially with strangers. She should know, he got his habit from her. Could her brother have found a friend so trustworthy that he confided in him?

"I like hearing about your family," Marc said. "Edgar is one of the best storytellers I have ever met. He keeps you riveted."

"It's a little secret called embellishment, but don't tell," Edgar replied.

"You never know, I may have a story or two up my sleeve," Marc said. His voice was so smooth and without judgment. It was as if he was part of the family.

"Anyway," Divina finally said. "You mean the time Claude broke the window you're sitting in?"

Edgar's eyes widened as his mind brought him back to that day, as his memories were as vivid as the things he saw around him through his own eyes. "He was what, three, Divina?"

"He just turned four," she replied.

Before the second story was finished, Divina wasn't just talking to

Edgar. Marc leaned in, his eyes fixed on her and Edgar when they spoke. He knew more about her family than she had imagined. With a little relief, she noticed instantly that the things he knew were the good times. Edgar must not have been able to let out the demons yet.

And they had painted a large, gleaming part of the wall.

Already, it was time to move on to the next part of the house.

Chapter 12

"I didn't plan on staying," Rebecca said to Claude quietly. She wanted to get her father's things and then leave on the next flight out. At least, originally. Walking back into the place, she wasn't sure why she felt so compelled to be consumed in it longer. Even if Claude hadn't been there, she still would have felt the tug to walk around, to touch the walls, and to sit in the middle of the floor.

"Maybe you need to rest," he said, still worried. She looked ready to topple over. The woman he remembered was there, right within his arm's length, but she was wrapped up in this new version of a person he had never met. Not only could he see she was a wife and a mother, but whatever was hurting her from the inside out, whatever her illness was doing to her, it was also crushing the light around her, coming in on her from the inches just beyond her skin.

"I am not going to stay here with you," she said pointedly. "I am very much in love with my family. I won't jeopardize it for anythi--"

"Shhh," he said to quiet her. "Don't assume. You need to rest. And maybe you need someone to listen to you. Someone who knows you--"

"My husband knows me," she snapped.

"I'm just saying, it's fine. We aren't going to pick up where we left off," he said, understanding it as he said it.

"I'm sorry. I'm just... I know."

"You can have my ear and my shoulder," he said as he went across the room. He cleared off his bed, which was covered in paper and a few lone canvasses. "My bed." She had stood up weakly and almost swaying with steps. She sat on his bed and gave him a knowing look. "I know," he answered her expression. "Don't even think about it. I'll take the floor."

It was strange now, funny how now he couldn't be there with her after the years. Understandable, but odd in the same thought. Claude sat on the floor as she put her head down on the pillow and crunched herself up into a ball on her side. While still on the floor, he reached up and pulled a blanket over her.

Rebecca, who looked instantly as if she had fallen asleep, said without much movement and with her eyes still closed, "I'm so scared."

He reached up again, brushed her shoulder and then clasped his hand around her arm. "A lot of people love you," he said. "And I'm right here." As her breaths became louder in sleep, he heard how hard it was for the air to come freely in and out of her lungs. It gripped him. He had been careful not to say that everything would be all right. He was scared that nothing would ever be all right again.

As if the years had melted, he watched her sleep as he had a thousand times before. She had what she wanted now. The stable husband with her own children was what she had left him for. Now, after all these years, she came back to the very spot she stood before she left.

He hadn't changed his life as she had. He never told her that while she went out to find all the things she needed in her life, he had been letting go of the one thing he had needed. Moving on had been the easy part, a relationship here and there, but it had been the constant reminders, which threw him for a loop. The pictures she sent he kept in a drawer and painted a painting for each one. There was always the lingering hope that she might come back, might want to see his paintings, might just want to see his face again. When his youth left, he even found himself hoping she had found all these things, led her full life, and then, before her life was over, she would come back to him. They would live the end of it together, in his loft, painting and sketching, because what they had was something most people never even get a taste of in their entire lives.

She wasn't old, though. And upon seeing her now, he knew she never would be old. Her face would look like that always because the few smile wrinkles would be all that aged her face. The color of her hair would never completely fade to gray. Instead of her living past her full life, she was going to die young. She was going to die before she could finish her full life.

Claude wasn't sure what to do or what words to say. He didn't know if holding her was wrong, if asking her questions would ultimately hurt her, if asking her to stay was going to make things worse. But he knew she had come here to gather her things, and maybe she wanted to see him. Deep down, she had always held on. She let go when she got what she had been searching for in her life, and now she had to look back not only on the fairy tale but those who were there before she found the answers to her dreams.

Claude had a feeling she had come back here to finish things, out of respect to him and to what they had, she had come to say goodbye.

Rebecca drifted into restless sleep, her body twisting, turning, her limbs thrashing about. Her eyes remained closed perfectly; the lids stretched thin over sight. Claude had never seen her sleep like this, not even when she had nightmares, not even when she was pushing back the things he asked but she couldn't yet find the courage to tell.

It wasn't long before he was studying her movements, searching her skin and her frame and her face for changes. The years had been long, and he couldn't tell what changes were due to age, to motherhood, to happiness, or to illness. Picking her apart with his eyes, he tried to separate which smile lines were from her children and which hardened lines were from the toll of her father's death. Claude had no real way to define such things, but he pretended all the same. It brought him a false sense of comfort. He wanted to sleep, to rest his eyes, but they refused his commands. He had to watch her every breath, careful, in case she stopped breathing. He watched her as parents watch their newborn on the first night, each breath a treasure, but the fear is there. They want to be the first to notice if the next breath doesn't come, the first to be able to run and get help.

Claude's gaze must have faltered for a lone, brief second. "Claude," whispered Rebecca, asking for him, wanting to know if he was there.

"Yeah, I'm right here," he said, bringing his face close to hers in the almost pitch black around them. Before he could censor his thoughts, he wondered if she had ever called out his name in night, in dream, when she had left him. He wondered if her husband knew he existed.

"Oh, Rebecca," he said softly as he fingered her hair around her face. Even in this darkness, her light colored face was visible. She seemed angelic and not of this world.

As if a few simple words drowning in his voice had broken her fever, she became still, the air pushing out of her lungs with too much energy to be healthy. Throughout the rest of her sleep, she did not turn nor say a word. She was as close to peace as she could be in this life. Claude remained a sculpture, perched at her bedside, eyes cemented into her as if during blinking she would disappear. For him, the night was long, but for her, it was the first time in memory when the pain didn't interrupt her sleep.

* * * * *

Little by little, strokes of paint and drops of sweat began to build back the devastation into the bigger picture. Rags became worse for wear, barely able to stay stitched together through holes and deepened stains. Skin was raked over by the sun, sharper in color and bronze. Not one of the three had a fingernail long enough to see over the tip of the finger. Divina had to cut blotches of paint out of her hair even though it was always tied back with a strip of elastic. The work was done on their hands, on their elbows, with their bodies tipped just beyond falling and their limbs reaching just to the point of pain.

When the earliest light became visible, Divina, Edgar, and Marc would be preparing to make their first lengths into the day. Just as evening set and the dark became so dense that no one could see their hands in front of their face, they would retreat to showers and sleep. The cycle continued seven days a week. Although tiring, the days weren't strenuous. There was an element of passion there, even in Marc who had no true ties to the place. A love for it was apparent with each move and each word.

Several trips of the large farm trucks carried away the debris from the steps of the great house. The pristine white was restored on the walls, inside and out, with at least three coats of paint. New lumber replaced the old planks of wood for floors and the porch. Glass windows were uniform and without cracks, shimmering, and completely see through. Just the mere light, which combed the rooms in the house, was amazing. Armed with large hedge clippers, they attacked the overzealous plant life surrounding the house. Roots of weeds and out of control vines were pulled from the ground. The leaves were trimmed, the flowering plants woven in between statues and fountains, and the lawn cut short. The sculptures were gone over with a fine toothcomb, cleaned with pieces of hand held fabric. Marc was especially good at this, his long thin fingers should have belonged to a pianist. He could reach in the most sullen of hidden areas. The result was almost alive, glistening pedestals with people and animals high above the ground. The pools and fountains found renewed water sources, and the muck, inches deep, was scrubbed out with bare hands.

When Divina and John married, flowers had been planted and a stone path set by hand. The area had been away from the house, so although livable, the conditions hadn't been seen close up. No one had been living there for some time when the renovations began. The place had closed up, swallowed itself. The flowers remained, a small area purified in the middle of the mess.

Marc came up with the idea quickly, obviously. The stone path should keep going, take the walker around the house, to all the doors, near all the fountains, up to all the statues. Diving into the dirt, the lawn was ripped apart, flowers planted tracing the sidewalk of stones. Magical and worthy of royalty, the house came together, the path smooth and warm, a heaven for bare feet. No jagged edges to hurt the sensitive skin; no unseen surprises in the surface to cause one to falter in their steps. The path was nearly too perfect to be made by people.

Most of the articles inside the house were discarded. Clothing was old and gnawed by moths. Furniture was rotting, and thinning curtains were see through. A few rooms were bathed with new carpet, rich and full, keeping imprints of feet after they stepped. Mostly, the rooms had floors of polished wood, slick and new, perfectly lined and measured. The cabinets were ripped from the wall and replaced with new wood, and the cracked tile of sinks and bathtubs was replaced with a jade and onyx marble.

Edgar proved to have magic in his hands. He carved new furniture, piece by piece, each leg seared with intricate designs, everything measured and then coated and sealed. Divina and Marc watched him in awe, his precision, his pure talent. Recognizing their inability, they merely offered to carry pieces or hold things while Edgar worked or sealed the wood. Many of the pieces were almost exactly the same as those which had been destroyed by age and neglect. Placing them in the house was like seeing the place new as it was before they were born, like taking a trip back in time to take a peak at how the rooms used to look.

There were some things that had survived the time. Dishes were cleaned and put in racks where they could be seen and admired and remembered, each distinct and different and holding onto their story. A cup here from the riverboat where their parents met, a plate there from their great grandmother's wedding, and many other pieces displayed coveted the prize of most treasured memory. Gold trinkets and decorations only needed to be cleaned to reclaim their natural luster. In the master bath, Divina found boxes made of marble, circles and rectangles with flower designs on the covers. Once cleaned, they shined as if they were made in the last few days. They were then returned to the new marble counters alongside the faucets. They almost spoke as if Rebecca was there, waiting for her to open them to retrieve a vital piece of jewelry or a swatch of make up.

Finishing touches added the character to the place. Grand sweeping curtains of red velvet lined the windows, seen slightly from the outside, and new towels with deeply intricate patterns were placed in the kitchen and bathrooms. The air in the house was full of light, more light than either child could remember from memories when they were young, and it smelled not of dust but of cleaner and flowers. Flowers, which were placed in old vases found everywhere from a bottom chest of drawers to near a tree in the front yard. Vases circled with detailed designs telling of people and cultures, of flowering vines and blossoming trees, of running horses and newly born butterflies. Each room was made up with live flowers in the corners, petals matching the colors in the rooms, from reds and blues to canary yellows. The rainbow was represented here.

The place was almost finished, and the hearts of the three people were evident in its cherished new state. Divina wasn't sure what she was going to do now to fill her time.

She barely saw John, which is not to say that she was the one always busy. Claude was in school, and Belinda had done what Divina had hoped for her. She was active in the nearby communities, traveling to the cities often, making friends with people of her own age and teaching skills like quilting and beading. Edgar had taken a test to get out of school, and after studying in the nights when he should have been sleeping, he passed it with flying colors. Now a few years ahead, he said he had time to figure out what he wanted and where he wanted to go. Meanwhile, cities were getting closer. This piece of property that Mr. Hamilton had been told would be the greatest asset of his life was becoming the greatest asset of John's life. They were no longer in the back roads as pavement and people began to appear regularly.

Divina had found her brother to be a great friend. Throughout the months of working on the house, he had proven to her who he had become, and although she would always love him unconditionally because he was her brother, she was now seeing she loved him as a person also. He was smart, quick thinking, and had more promise than even she had imagined. Marc was always there, by Edgar's side, and within the first month of working, by her side. He was there in case she needed a hand. Reaching in quickly and without thought, he had saved her from many disastrous situations like falling debris or slippery cement or sharp edges of hidden tools. Probably from being with Edgar, Marc learned quickly which buttons to push in Divina to make her laugh, to make her relax. The result was calm, and work was fun.

Each story told brought them all in together as if sharing a secret, and while during some of the days when it rained, the secrets became as dark as the clouds, each one instead of staying silent, huddled together and built up a tower of united strength. The house reflected this.

Unknowingly tossed aside deep in a closet, a broken framed painting lay in wait.

On the very last day, as Divina walked through her old room admiring a quilted comforter Belinda had made for her on her bed, she opened the closet door. Confused for a moment, she pulled it out into the light. She held the unattractive painting in her arms, close, smelling the dust on it. Edgar came in and recognized it immediately.

"Mom loved that thing," he remarked, gazing at it with curiosity.

"Do you think it is pretty," Divina asked him.

"Wow," Marc said with great appreciation as he entered the room and saw the painting.

"Don't tell me you like this," Edgar said to him.

"It's amazing. Can't you see it," Marc asked.

"See what," Divina asked quizzically.

"Right there. Here, just look at it right. There's a red woman right here, not even a real woman, but more of the essence of a great woman. Probably the artist's mother or lover," Marc explained, touching the canvas colors gently.

"You got that from *this*?" Edgar didn't hide the surprise in his voice.

A soft expression covered Divina's features. "I see," she said, quietly, but with a surge of sweetness. The thought never occurred to Divina that this woman was actually her mother. She figured Rebecca had seen the piece, recognized a common bond with the picture, felt a connection with the essence described because it was so purely part of her.

Tracing the frame of the red woman's face with a finger, Marc knelt close to Divina. "She reminds me very much of you," he said to her.

Her eyes fell down, like a curtain closing. "Thank you," she replied, genuinely feeling the connection with Rebecca.

"Okay," Edgar said sarcastically. "Whatever you guys say."

"Let me take this for a few days," Marc said. "I'll have it as good as new."

"Thanks, it was my mother's," Divina replied.

"I'll protect it with my life," Marc said, understanding the sentiment of the painting.

The three left the house, Marc carrying the large painting under his arm. As Divina stood on the very top of the stairs, she turned and looked at the house. The other two stopped on their way down the stairs to look at her curiously. Then, with her head held high, and her eyes wise, she looked out over the land, over the lawn and trees and sky, and then, finally, down the steps at Marc and Edgar.

"What is it," Edgar asked her. Divina's eyes still were large and wide, clouded with a far away look. "It's as if she is looking at the place for the first time," Edgar said with confusion to Marc.

Nodding briefly before turning to go, Marc took one step down before saying a word. "Maybe she is," he said seriously.

Edgar followed behind his friend, pretending to understand. When they were out of Divina's hearing range, Edgar couldn't help but ask Marc more questions. "What was that all about?"

"Why don't you ask her," Marc asked, shaking his head with a smile.

"You know her now as well as I do," Edgar replied.

"I highly doubt that."

"But it's true."

Walking with their matching strides, Marc was quiet for a moment. Edgar was beginning to wonder if he would speak again, if his answer would only be the silence.

"She's born in that ground, in the walls of that house. The floors may be new, and the windows, and the paint, but the shell is the same. That used to be your mother's house, your father's house, and now, I think she's realized she's made it hers," Marc said slowly, deliberately.

"You got all that from that glazed look in her eyes?"

Marc laughed. "Well, her eyes are very expressive."

Edgar shook his head and rolled his eyes jokingly. "She doesn't even live in that house."

"That doesn't matter," Marc said very quietly. "Watch the way she touches things in those rooms, especially things that belonged to your mother. To her, everything is breakable and has great meaning as if the objects were still a direct link to your mother's life."

Edgar paused in his walking, thinking deeply about the words. "You're absolutely right. All the things my mother loved are the things that Divina was so careful to save and clean and put back out."

"She's strong, hardened. Probably the toughest woman I've ever met," Marc said.

"That's a nice way of putting it. Just say what you mean. She's a tomboy."

"No, she's not. Maybe when she was younger she was, but not since I've known her." Marc laughed a little at an approaching memory. "When I first met her, I was worried she would hurt herself, just running through the woods like that from John's house."

Edgar smiled. He knew Divina would never hurt herself in the woods, not even if she lost her sight. She could listen, feel her way through the darkness. As protective as Edgar was of his sister, he never worried about her in the woods. Divina knew how to handle herself, how to move and keep safe.

"I know better now," Marc said, a full smile playing instantly on his lips. "Much better now."

The two walked again in stride, Edgar, with his long legs almost disproportional to his body, and Marc, holding the painting under his arm and still owning some sort of balance in his agility and youth.

Divina stood on the top of the stairs for what seemed like an eternity. Honestly, she didn't know if she waited there for seconds, moments, or hours. Edgar and Marc were long gone when she descended her throne, each step a masterful achievement. She had promised herself one day that this would happen. For the first time since her parents' death, she knew that they were proud of her. This was something they would have been proud to have seen her do. The place was beautiful, functioning, and alive again. Birds were already visiting the fountain, and the flowers filled every crevice of what used to be dark and dusty. Beneath the new white paint, and in the dirt set with stones, and within the very walls, which surrounded the rooms, the house was singing.

* * * * *

Claude had coffee brewing a few inches from the foot of the bed, the pot resting easily on the floor. When Rebecca woke, the smell infiltrated her nostrils and made her smile. She stretched her arms lazily over her head, making her elbows form a line instead of an angle. Without a word, Claude poured her a cup.

"It's your brand and mocha," Claude said, the pitch of his voice going higher when he said the last word.

"You hate mocha," she replied, her eyes still clogged from sleep.

"Doesn't matter. I had some around."

"You keep my coffee on hand?"

Claude didn't bother to lie or explain. "Yes."

Truth be told, he hated mocha. She had loved it, the way it filled her. She swore she could feel it in her bloodstream within fifteen minutes after drinking it. During the last several years, he had been drinking it. Inside, even though he winced at every first swallow in the morning, he told himself he had grown a taste for it.

"How are you feeling," Claude asked her.

The whole structure in her face seemed to change. It was as if his words had physically hit a button, which took all the oxygen out of her body. She had almost forgotten. Her eyes seemed to deepen in her face before his very eyes. Rebecca glanced at her hands again, a habit she had picked up since she last saw him. The diversion worked at avoiding the nervousness that comes with staring.

"It's strange here," she said. "I forget I left, forget I'm sick, forget I have people waiting for me. I remember within seconds; it never lasts more than a few brief seconds. Never moments."

"I'm sorry," Claude said to her, unsure whether he was referring to her sickness or her remembering or her forgetting. If she wanted an apology for any of those things, he figured she could take it from his words.

Rebecca scoffed, her hand giving him a short wave. Her gesture told him not to be silly, not to feel bad about things he had no control over.

Claude smiled, as he knew the routine she went through in the morning. Her eyes began to widen, to become more heavily absorbed with the light. The hardened lines around her mouth began to soften, to smooth out like they were being sanded. This morning, the lines softened around her eyes, and near the tips of her eyebrows, but the smoothness didn't come. The sheet indentations from how her body was shaped when she slept were beginning to fade. He inhaled deeply, but not with such strength that it would cause attention. He didn't want to explain that she had the same fragrance, that lingering of the perfume she had been wearing the day before mixed with her salon shampoo and skin softening lotion. The smells had lost their newness due to the time they had covered her skin, but the remaining scent was distinctly sweet.

The woman before him may not be the same girl he had loved, but she was housed in the same shell with the same essence. She had traveled a long journey, both inside and on the road, and now she was here again. The fog in his brain began to lift, and Claude suddenly was hit with the revelation. He knew why she had come back, and it wasn't for a few miscellaneous items. Rebecca carried a tremendous weight on her back now, one so strenuous that she nearly toppled over with each step forward. She hadn't come here for a few scattered memories of her father. Claude knew she had come back because she needed to forget.

Rebecca sipped at her mocha, letting the steam come off it as if the colorless swirls were dancing. She liked it when it burned going down her throat, feeling the warm liquid slide down all the way to her stomach. Claude didn't let on that he knew why she was there. Perhaps she didn't even know. Putting her on the spot may cause her to flee, and although he wasn't sure how to make the pain go away, he would try any way she asked.

"What time is it," she asked him suddenly.

Claude scrambled about, tossing and turning a few blankets and other objects, looking for the small clock he kept in case he needed an alarm. He had learned to live with time to mean nothing. Finally, he found it under a wadded up pair of paint-splattered jeans.

He handed her the clock. The hour was early still, and the morning young, but she sat straight up and poised herself as if she was ready to run out the door.

"I have a flight to catch," she said to him. He hadn't been expecting that, and the surprise raced across his features. Trying to quickly recover, he pushed his jolted feelings aside.

Rebecca hadn't been prepared to say what she wanted to say, to ask what she wanted to ask. There was a stillness in the waters inside her.

"You could catch a later flight," he said.

"No," she said, shaking her head. "They'll worry."

"Of course," he replied, quietly, never having the luxury of forgetting like she did.

The word mother could have been tattooed across her forehead, and it still would have paled in comparison with her parental face and smile.

"But…" she began, not wanting to ask, but dreaming she could. Dreams were few and far between these days. Dreams used to get her through, make her keep going, and now she was learning that the days ahead holding the bright spot of light resembling her dreams were fading. The time for dreaming was something Rebecca could no longer afford.

Claude's attention was stapled to whatever she was going to say.

"I want to come back," she said, quickly adding, "if that's all right. If it's not--"

"Anytime, as long as you want. I'll even meet you if you can't come back here. Name the place," Claude said, interrupting her, running his sentences together too quickly to be seen as calm.

Her eyes darted down again. The man who never wanted to leave the loft and wouldn't take her anywhere now was willing to do it all. Before she could censor herself, a smile sprinted lightly on her lips. The guilt was already preparing to linger in her heart.

No matter what she told herself, she felt low, and the ultimate betrayal was on her fingertips. She could convince herself a hundred times over that this was comfort from a friend, this was a piece of her past that brought her some calm, but if the situation was reversed, and her husband did this under these same conditions, she knew she wouldn't understand. Within that spark, she wondered if she was as brave as she once thought, if she had the courage to tell him. Because not telling him would be worse than anything she could ever do.

Chapter 13

John was waiting up for her. He had heard from the rumbling of the farm that today was the day the house was finished. Finally. Now, things could get back to how they were supposed to be.

Divina had put everything into this project. That was what it was: a project. John hadn't expected the late nights, the long hours, the mornings when she would be long gone before he even entered his last dream of the night. He certainly hadn't expected her to work seven days a week. She didn't even take the weekends off. But the few times he saw her, he saw her as he had never seen her in all her life. The determination and passion was incredible. She truly loved transforming the old place, and she did every detail, every part by her own very hands. She could have bought new quilts, but instead she patched the old ones and cleaned them, taking what would have been a trip into town and making it a long, tedious job. He had been putting the wife things aside, for now. There had been no talk of children.

Sad as he was that he felt as he did, he knew if he would have been able to see how this project was done and how long it took, he never would have given her permission or money to do it. John knew after the first week he should have hired someone else to come in and do it. Originally, the expense was what stopped him, but while he worked and came home to an empty house, he began to think the money would have been well spent.

Sitting at the kitchen table, peeling an apple, he waited for Divina to come home under dim light. He heard her long before he saw her. As quiet as she was, he had trained his ears. To a common stranger, the only sound was rustling leaves bitten by breeze, but to John, he could hear each individual footstep coming closer.

The screen door slammed shut behind Divina as she stepped inside.

"Welcome home," John said, getting up to give her a hug.

"Thanks," she said, instinctively backing away from him. His face told her he wasn't happy with her retreating, and his expression questioned her. "I need a shower and some sleep. We finished today," she said as she left the room, the last sentence stretching out as her face turned away from him.

"I know," he said after her, unsure whether she was in the vicinity to hear him anymore.

With that, she went down the hall, locked the bathroom door, and began to run the water, waiting for the cold to become warm and welcoming. He had said she had come home, and while she slept here and got her mail at this address, she felt her room was not in this house. It was through the trees, and up the grand stairs, and surrounded with large, clear windows. She missed her old bed.

The cascading water, clear and sticky wet, fell from the showerhead. She took a long shower, dragging out the moments, letting the water take away the dirt and dust, the paint and debris. Going through the rituals, her motions were mechanic but sloping. She brushed her teeth for a few more minutes than usual, brushed her hair with a few more strokes, and rubbed the lotion on her hands long after it became invisible. John would be asleep by now.

Tiptoeing with great ease and practice, she knew which places in the hall creaked and which would not betray her sunken feet with sound. No lights were turned on. The bathroom light was turned off long before she dared unlock the door. The bedroom door showed a crack of darkness also. The space was too small to slip through, so she knew the door would squeak when she entered the room. There was a choice now. Move quickly, so the sound moved with a rapid speed and hope it doesn't cut the silence enough to wake him, or move slowly, and let the sound drift longer as if crying in pain.

Divina decided to move quickly. With one fluid step, she was inside, and the door's voice sliced off. John's silhouette didn't move. She slipped into bed, far from his side, and she closed her eyes, careful not to breathe too loudly.

Her empty thoughts kept her up until she thought of Mary. Tomorrow, the house would see its first sunrise fully restored. Mary had promised to be there; she wanted to see it. The woman hadn't been out since the beginning of the renovations. Her illness kept her in with ups and downs but was beginning to leave her in the bad spots more than the good. Divina would take her out there, show her around, see her smile. Even when Claude visited from school, Mary had trouble smiling. It seemed to hurt her.

With beautiful thoughts of the coming day, Divina fell into a deep sleep.

John heard her come in, the softened sounds she made when she tried so hard to be quiet. He used to cherish the noises, thinking she cared so much that she didn't want to wake him. Now, he was beginning to wonder if she was so quiet because she didn't want to face him. No, he'd never believe that. Things like that could never happen to him, not with his wife. John looked forward to the morning, reaching over and finding the emptiness filled with her sweet slumber.

The morning was still dark when John fell asleep. When he woke on this first day with Divina's job done, he reached over. And she was gone.

Mary had been prepared for her outing, and Divina had walked with a spring in her step all the way to the building in which Mary was being taken care of. The old woman's face had a large smile, despite a hidden wince, and there was such joy and anticipation.

Divina had gathered Edgar and Marc to help with Mary. The three helped wheel her out and held onto her oxygen tank and other necessary devices. With all the help, the situation went smoothly and without pain. The four began the journey to the old house.

"How is John," Mary asked Divina, her face scrunched up.

"He's good," she replied simply and without much thought.

"I suppose now you are about to embark on the real part of the marriage," Mary said, almost to herself. Marc and Edgar remained quiet, watching their steps carefully as if each held more fascination than it truly did. They weren't going to get into this.

"I thought my marriage was going very well,' Divina said.

"Of course, you never see him," Edgar replied under his breath.

Mary's eyes widened in agreement, and she merely pointed a finger at Edgar and shook it in an animated gesture. Edgar had the right idea, the same frame of thought as she did.

Marc was sure not to speak.

"Don't worry about me, Mary," Divina said, her voice dipped in patience. The conversation about John was over, and all four of them knew it.

Edgar felt the need to lighten the mood and took it upon himself to bring up a new subject. "Mary, you should have seen Divina when she was trying to drag all that stuff down from the attic."

Marc laughed out loud, sharing the memory. "She wasn't paying attention to anything that may be above her, so she started dragging all these beams..."

Mary was engrossed, the story lively and about Divina. It was just one of the small things that had happened and made everyone laugh during the day. Divina had been paying attention to the bottom half of the beams, and not the actual weight of the full pressure, so when she lifted them, they nearly toppled over on her from feet above her head.

"She was like a stick, perfectly straight, and about to fall over completely stiff and on her back, with a bunch of vertical beams about to fall over on her," Edgar said, his eyes dancing wildly.

"How did you get out of that mess," Mary asked, now wondering if she should have been worried while Divina was out doing all these renovations.

Edgar patted Marc's shoulder.

Marc pretended to take a bow while holding onto the equipment which came with Mary. He succeeded playfully and with a surprising amount of grace. "No big deal. I just ran over and helped push them away from her and balance them."

"Good thing he was there," Mary said pointedly to Divina.

"No kidding. And this sort of thing happened all the time. That was Marc's job, you know, making sure I didn't get myself killed."

"A regular guardian angel," Mary said with a smile, warming to the new face among the siblings.

"I wouldn't go that far," Marc answered, somewhat shyly. "Anyone would have done the same."

The stories continued, and Marc captivated Mary with how much he knew about these kids which she considered her own blood, and his knack for storytelling left the other two only speaking to fill in a few of the details.

Turning a corner, the house came into view. Mary actually gasped, and she was speechless.

"Mary, are you all right," Edgar asked, his voice high and words rapid, fear tracing his eyes.

"It looks so beautiful. There is no question. The glory that was there before has returned," she said, her hand shaking slightly. No one knew whether it was from the emotion or the illness.

"Do you want us to give you the grand tour, Ma'am?"

"Call me Mary," she said to Marc.

"Whatever you want, Ma'--I mean, Mary."

The woman's eyes were off him by then, surveying the grounds, the house, the gleam.

It truly was a place she had once walked, a place she remembered well.

With every blink, every small turn of her neck, she saw one more beautiful memory. The fountains were spraying, the sculptures shining, the paint reflecting the sunlight. Many things were even better than before like the stone paths, but the flowers, the flowers were the same wild and free and alive, nearly breathing.

"Take me inside," Mary said, her voice trembling with excitement.

Slowly, through each room, showing each detail, the three took Mary around the house. She responded with such joy, even at the smallest things like the clean marble boxes that belonged to Rebecca in the master bath.

"I'm sorry," Mary whimpered, eyes welling up. "I don't know why this is so emotional."

The old woman reached out and grabbed the nearest hand, which was Marc's. He was surprised but gently touched. Edgar shrugged his shoulders as he drew in a breath. Even as a little boy, before his parents were gone, he had never known how to act in situations so emotional like this. Grasping Marc's hand tighter and tighter, Mary noticed Divina kneel down to look at her eye level.

"You're home, that's why," Divina said to her, and Mary felt the light in the young woman's eyes, warm and brilliant.

Mary let Marc's hand go without realizing it to grab onto Divina's hands and pull them to her cheek. The tour went on as they shared old memories and made new ones.

* * * * *

Rebecca returned home after seeing Claude. She took the flight that she had booked, but it was in the airport that she bought the other tickets that would bring her back. It was the first time ever that Claude had taken her to the airport. She partly believed he only went because he was worried about her health, that she might faint or need to be taken to the hospital. Claude left after she was settled in and waiting for the flight to be announced over the intercom.

That was when the trips began. The first year, there were only two. Although the rest were few and far between, they grew as time passed.

Rebecca never stayed long, a few days at the most each time. Somehow, the shorter the time, the less the betrayal. The same reasons she had come to love him in the first place were still there. She watched him paint.

They were both careful, as if in on a special secret. They slept alone but in the same room. There was nothing more than a kiss on the cheek when she arrived at his door. Rebecca could not let it go farther than that, no matter how much she loved him. Claude listened to her tell stories of her children, beautiful raging stories of these people who came from inside of her and ran around in the world now. He could picture them in his mind if he tried. She spoke of Mr. Hamilton often, his soft face and worried eyes.

Claude knew from the way she spoke of them that she loved them. They were her life. They were the life that she left him to find.

Both of them knew that she never would leave her family. Rebecca had them as her foundation, but they were wobbly, needing so much from her. Her children needed to be taught, to be loved, to see her and hug her and play and hear her read to them. Her husband needed his wife to get better, needed the woman he married to be there when he was old and gray. Who would find his keys when he lost them? Who would tell him his socks didn't match his pants when he had an important meeting? She was being drained already, and they loved her with their whole hearts, but there was nothing they could do to soothe the pain.

Claude didn't need anything from her. He listened without saying judgmental words. Rebecca had almost forgotten how well he knew her, the ins and outs and secrets and past and dreams. He knew it all. She had been searching for understanding, for someone to understand what she felt and needed and wanted to express. Claude could never fully know the extent of what was in the thoughts, which she never said out loud, but the words and way she acted was enough. He understood.

She had never been afraid to live, but now, she was shuddering in her sleep at her approaching end. Claude knew she thought she couldn't leave this life because she wasn't done. It had nothing to do with her. Her family needed her, and she couldn't let them down. Just keep holding on until the kids are grown, until Mr. Hamilton learns how to be independent again.

When her bones hurt on the inside, and when blinking caused an incurable ache, she had to go breathe the old air. Her thoughts jumbled with a prognosis, sometimes good and sometimes devastating, and then she would leave. Speaking to Claude was a way to hear herself, to fully comprehend what was happening. She left with a sense of herself and a confidence. Flying out and coming back in what seemed like moments, Claude painted less and waited more. Some visits were promising, her pain not evident, and others were crumbling, where she shouldn't have been traveling at all. He was the ear who listened to her abandoned soul and the healer of the wounds which doctors knew nothing about.

Mr. Hamilton never argued, although he suspected. When she returned from these trips, it was as if she had been given a drug to bring up her level of hope. She was stronger, clearer in what she wanted and needed to do. If whatever she was doing made her feel like this, then he would never say a word against it although it broke him inside.

Because he never questioned or asked, she never told him that there was no secret lover who magically made her alive again. Maybe that is a good thing because there was no need to tell Mr. Hamilton that she traveled so long just so someone would listen to her ramble on and on. That would hurt him even more than what he assumed. The wife he loved flew across the nation because he couldn't listen to her.

A year came when Rebecca got better. In that year, it was as if she had never been sick at all. Mr. Hamilton thought it was over. She didn't go on any surprise trips that year. Even the children thought that their mother was simply fixed, simply healthy.

Rebecca knew better, felt it within her. This wasn't the sort of thing that just goes away. This was a gift from something more powerful. Now, she had a chance to make the last parts the best, to not bring forth the pain on her family. They didn't have to watch her wither.

The children played and ran with her. Rebecca was up at dawn and went to sleep late in the night. She read books, drew sketches. The garden became a sanctuary, a place of the most divine refuge. She loved the flowers, grew them, cut them, braided them into her hair like a hippie. Mr. Hamilton took her to formal gatherings. The two looked as they did in the beginning, strong and ready to take on the world. Only now, they had taken on the world, and they had won, and now they were just staying at the top. She felt strong and wise, her body free of most of the pain she had known. Her mind was sharp and quick, decisive.

For that period of time, she didn't need Claude. He understood. He was the one who was there when she was weak, but when she was strong, she wanted to be with them.

She visited once in that year, just to check up on him.

"So, you're better," he asked her.

It was hard to tell him. She hadn't even told her family. In her gut, all along, she had known what was there in the beginning was still there, looming, waiting for her to wrap up her life, to finish things, to prepare.

"I am feeling well right now, yes. But it won't be long before I am sick again," she said.

"Maybe... You don't know. Miracles happen all the time. I read about them in the paper and think of you," he said as if this was a natural outcome.

"I know, though. I know," she said, the wisdom of knowing herself better than he did for once flowing over their conversation. He knew then that she had felt it, a prick of pain here, a jolt of abnormal stress there. She felt it coming.

That was the night he sat next to her on his bed and held her until she had to catch her flight. His arms were warm but strangely unfamiliar. She felt as if she had never been there at all. Even the mere air changed on that night.

A month after she returned home from that visit with Claude, she grew very sick.

Mr. Hamilton raced her to the hospital, and by the time she came out from the care unit, his eyes were red from lack of sleep.

The news was a surprise. It was a shocking, stunning discovery that had everyone involved dumbfounded.

Rebecca wasn't relapsing.

She was pregnant.

* * * * *

Divina had been sensing John's impatience for the past months. Not knowing how or when to bring it up, she simply discarded it. Before work on the house began, she probably would have asked him about it, done whatever she could to please him. Now, she couldn't. It was just too tiring, and she couldn't just be the wife anymore.

The severity was evident when Belinda came bounding up the grand stairs during Mary's tour of the house. "Divina, John wants you to come back to the house right away," Belinda said with no urgency in her voice.

"Why? What's happened?"

"Nothing," Belinda said to her, shaking her head.

"Oh. Well, do you want to finish the tour with us," Divina asked, her pride bruised by John despite his physical absence.

Belinda smiled warmly. Of course she did.

They came to one of the last rooms, Rebecca's old study. The place looked almost identical to how it did in the past. The desk was even messy in the same way.

"Wow," Belinda commented. "It's practically identical. But there is something off..."

"The painting is gone," Mary said to her.

"The one with the red woman," Marc asked.

"That's it! How did you know," Mary asked him, surprised he knew something only the family should have known.

"I'm having it cleaned and redone. It was quite a mess, but it really is a great piece above everything," Marc replied.

Belinda was deathly quiet although no one noticed. She had been keeping Claude in the back of her mind for many, many years.

Rebecca and Belinda had been estranged for most of their lives. When Divina was born, Belinda and Rebecca reconciled. The women weren't together often although Belinda was often around. She was a socialite. The woman was involved in practically every organization in the communities nearby. Belinda was basically a caregiver to the children whenever they needed watching, but when they didn't, she was nowhere to be found. It was natural that she stayed permanently in the light of all that occurred. She had been a widower for many years and had no children of her own.

The sisters had come together in the end, during the last months when Rebecca was at her worst. Belinda knew all about Claude. She doubted Mr. Hamilton knew Claude even existed.

"I always thought it was hideous, but she loved that piece," Belinda said quietly, almost unaware the words had materialized from her thoughts.

"I know," Divina said. "Do you know why?" The question was point blank, and Divina believed her aunt would never lie to her. She had no reason to because this seemed a polite conversation, and a simple answer surely would explain everything.

"That is a story for another time," Belinda said, trying to mask her face from the sadness that crept up into it from her throat.

Although Belinda's tone was odd, they all let it pass by without another thought. They continued their tour, and then they began back to the house where John waited for Divina.

Laughter echoed through the trees and hit John's ears before he could see their shadows on the grass. He was standing, waiting for them. The crowd saw John, and as if they were birds suddenly being shooed away, they dispersed, leaving Divina standing there.

"You weren't there this morning," he said with disappointment.

"John, when was the last morning I was there?"

"But you finished the house."

"I took Mary over. I told you. I made her a promise," Divina said, and she was unsure why she felt so defensive over this small insignificant situation.

"That was the last time I wake up when you won't be there," he said, the words not a question but harboring the tension of a threat.

With that, John turned in silence and walked back in the house. The screen door slammed behind him, and it sounded so angry. Only John could make a door, which normally causes a thunderous noise, to sound even angrier.

Before Divina could think, could comprehend the weight of that statement, she found herself standing perfectly still. There was an element of shock to it. Her blood felt cold. Just when she thought that maybe things would be all right, that she could have a life, John had let her know that the last few months were a one time thing. She knew the freedom she had been feeling was being taken away, and just as surely as if he had tied a rope to her when he stood there, she felt herself being dragged into the house after him.

The night resulted in silence as John didn't speak to her. His anger was magnified in the way he did some business filing and flipping through paper work. Movements were razor sharp and had loud, booming voices.

Belinda came in quietly to check on Divina.

"How are you?"

"Fine," Divina replied dryly, biting the invitation to talk badly about John. Instead, she decided to change the subject. "Tell me about the painting? Where did Mom buy it?"

"Buy it," Belinda asked, quickly thinking that she wished her sister had bought it.

Things would have been much more simple. "She didn't buy it."

"It was given to her? Wow."

"Actually, a... friend of hers painted it."

"Seriously? Who?"

"It was a friend she had known very well for a long time. The painting wasn't just a gift. It was of her. She's the red woman."

Divina took this all in, angry with herself for not liking the painting in the beginning.

"Do I know the artist," Divina asked with such joy. Her mother invoked so much emotion that one of her friends had decided to capture it on canvas.

"No, he's an old friend from long before you were born."

"He. What kind of friend are we talking about here?"

"Oh, Divina. You know your mother loved your father more than anything in the world," Belinda said, escaping the truth between the lines. She had yet to say anything untrue.

"What's his name?"

Belinda paused a long time, not wanting to tell her. His signature on the painting was messy and impossible to read. Finally, she answered, and she stared at Divina because she wanted to catch the look on her face, even if it lasted only a moment.

Belinda's reply was given without a trace of any emotion that may cause curiosity. "I don't remember."

Chapter 14

Rebecca was pregnant. Part of her rejoiced while the other wept. The doctors told her she shouldn't have the child. It would be weak; she wouldn't provide a good home for its development.

Mr. Hamilton worried the strain would break his wife, be too much for her. "I don't want you to do this," he said to her.

"I'm going to go soon anyway," she said.

Rebecca wanted this baby. It was inside her, sharing her heartbeat. As impossible it may be to understand, she already loved it. She could hold on for a few more years, see the first steps and hold the baby when it cried. More than anything, she wanted another baby now that she had one in her. Before she found out she was pregnant, she hadn't even considered it, but now that it happened, it seemed like a great blessing.

"I really want this baby," she said to her husband.

"I know," he answered, stroking her hair. "You know I would love another child, another little piece made from you and me, but I don't want anything to happen to you. We need you. Divina, Edgar, and I all do."

"It's such a miracle," she said, rubbing her flat belly, imagining it as it would swell and become large with child. "I didn't know I could be filled with such infinite hope."

Mr. Hamilton saw the change in his wife, the way her whole spirit was renewed with the news of the baby. Inside, he was petrified, but he hadn't seen her this happy since before she first got sick. She was so brilliant and radiant with enthusiasm. Promising she'd eat right and take great care of herself, she convinced him that there was no choice. They were going to have a baby.

On the drive home, the couple was armed with directions and rules that Rebecca would have to follow to stay healthy. The next eight months were going to be tough, but she laughed so full and talked so fast that Mr. Hamilton almost believed that this was going to fix everything.

"It's going to be a boy," she said to him as he drove, his eyes cautiously scanning the area out the windshield. There was no way he would miss something which might jeopardize her health if he got into an accident.

Before Rebecca, he barely stopped at stop signs. He thought they were more of a tip than a law. Now, not only did he slow down, he stopped completely and well behind cross walks. Then, he looked both ways at least four times. He wasn't prepared to sacrifice anything now, not when what was next to him was so precious and being threatened.

"I suppose you have a name all picked out," he said sarcastically.

"As a matter of fact..."

Mr. Hamilton actually glanced over at her, surprised and trying to discover if she was being serious. His eyes automatically switched back over to the road. "You're not kidding," he said seriously.

She straightened her back, slightly moved her frame so that she was facing his driver's side window. Her hair touched the ceiling of the car, and the vents blew air that made the loose strands whirl in motion. She sat with on leg crossed under the other, a model of excitement evident in her pose.

"Do you want to hear it," she asked him, her voice practically bubbling over.

"Yeah, sure."

"Claude," she said, rolling it off her tongue, letting it roll down the dashboard like dice.

"Like the painter," he asked. He shook his head a little, then a little more, and tapped his finger on the steering wheel. She could see it grow on him immediately. He liked it. "That's a pretty famous name," he commented.

"I just really like that name," she said.

"Claude. Like the painter," he said again. Although he was referring to Monet and didn't even know there was another Claude in Rebecca's life, the name felt right. There was no warning or nerves that came along with her idea. It suited the baby soon to come.

Finally, she said softly, "Yeah, just like the painter."

He drove on, contemplating naming his son after a man who died long ago and lived to be a legend, a man who had such a talent that God himself must have reached down and kissed his hands.

Rebecca sat beside him, letting the name rumble like thunder in her mind's quiet. She was naming her son after a man who she loved, who she loved long before she had married, who painted. She was naming him for a passion that never ended although it was kept in secret even from her own husband.

That was the last time they spoke of names. If Claude had been born a girl, the baby probably would have still been named Claude out of respect for Rebecca's wishes.

The night Claude was born was truly one of the greatest and most tragic nights of the Hamilton household.

* * * * *

Divina sat up straight in bed, drenched in sweat, hair matted to her face. She had felt it unlike anything that had ever happened in her life. She threw the thin covers off and hit the bare floor with bare feet running.

John didn't stir.

Clad in a white tank top, which graced her legs a few inches above her knees, she ran down the steps and through the grass that was slick and wet with dew. Divina's eyes weren't used to the dark, but she relied on the skills from her youth, taking in the light ahead of her and going toward it while avoiding whatever may be in her way.

She threw open the door with all her might. If she had looked harder through her blurry eyes, she would have seen that all the lights were on in the building.

Edgar was rubbing his eyes and walking slowly, still in a daze from sleep. The bright lights had filtered through his window and woken him up. He saw his sister running wildly, madly, and he knew instinctively. In that instant, he was completely awake.

When she reached the room, Edgar was at her heels. The dimness in the eyes of all the people in the blinding room of light was enough to tell them.

"She didn't feel any pain," one of the doctors said as she came closer.

Divina didn't hear them, didn't care what they had to say. It was what they weren't saying that was going to be the thing to make today the someday that would change everything. The someday that we all wish would never come. She went straight into her room, knelt down until their faces were inches from one another. Edgar stood beside his sister, gently placing his hand on her back. She lay still, eyes closed. Mary was gone.

People filtered in and out of the room. Divina didn't hear or feel Edgar leave and come back with a chair. He took the strength of his arms and forced her muscles to sit on the chair near the bed. She barely felt movement in her joints. Then, Edgar left again. He went and talked to doctors. By the time the sun was up, Edgar had made the majority of the arrangements, so his sister didn't have to have that on her hands. He did it as much for her as for Mary.

John woke up, reached over in confidence. She had corroded his last nerve. He felt the temperature rise. Staying in a white tee shirt and sweatpants, he left the house in search for his missing wife.

Edgar had just returned from making the last of the phone calls when John burst through the door.

"Where is Divina," he asked Edgar with a voice as rough as sandpaper.

"She's in there, but--" Edgar didn't get to finish his sentence because John was already out of the room. The protective layer in Edgar's skin was instantly awakened as he followed John as quickly as he could.

Divina was in the hallway. It was the first time she had stood up in hours.

"What the hell are you doing," John yelled. He didn't notice the swelling of the tears from her mourning or the tracks, which were left behind from all the tears that had already escaped.

"Back off, John," Edgar warned, jumping in between John and Divina, staring straight into John's eyes.

John then made the wrong move by pushing Edgar aside and clearing a path to Divina. Edgar, although as tall as John now, was much thinner and moved without much of a shove, but he bounced back with a vengeance. His reflexes were impeccable.

Edgar came up swinging and nearly knocked John off his feet. Marc came in at this moment to see why everyone was near the building. He ran and grabbed Edgar, pulling him away from John. John was ready to fight back, but saw Marc's eyes and decided against it.

Angry and bitter, Divina shoved past the group of them towards the door outside.

She brushed up against John as she walked through, her face near his, and in a low voice laced with poison, she said, "Mary died last night."

Divina stopped for a moment a few feet from John, waiting to see his reaction, his embarrassment.

She got a reaction, but it surprised the whole room. "Then you should have woken me up. There is no excuse, Divina," he said, the chill in the air growing every moment.

Without a word or a second's contemplation, she left the building. Divina was positive if she exploded at John right now and said all she'd been thinking, their marriage would never survive it.

Marc physically still had Edgar pinned, and he picked him up, and placed him facing in the opposite direction away from John and towards where his sister had left. Marc knew Edgar well enough to feel his shaking, his need to go back at John. Instead, the diversion worked, and Edgar left the building.

Marc followed behind, looked back at John a few times on his way out. This man was supposed to be his boss. Right now, all he saw was an unbelievable human being. Upon stepping outside, Marc saw Edgar pacing nearby.

"Marc, I have to go and make the last of the arrangements. I don't want Divina to do it, but I can't just leave her."

"I'll stay with her until you get back," his friend promised.

"I saw her walk toward the barn where we're keeping the new calves," Edgar said. With that, he turned and walked toward the house, keeping his eyes glued to the ground. He didn't want to accidentally see John right now. He didn't trust himself enough to believe he would keep walking.

The strip of white light from the opening door made a growing line in the barn. Divina sat on some hay bales that were piled in a corner. Her head was in her hands, but she wasn't crying. She was viciously running her fingers through her hair again and again.

Marc walked the distance quickly between them and sat next to her. "Divina," he said, trying to see her face, which was still buried in her hands.

"I'm fine," she said, the words muffled and hard to understand, but he made them out. The hint was obvious; she wanted him to leave. She thought she needed to be alone, but Marc knew better. She could kick him out, but he would just sit on the ground a few feet away from her.

Instead, Marc put an arm around her. He didn't say a word. He lowered his head until it was at the same level as hers. He sat there while she started to cry, truly and wholly sob. For a few minutes, she had kept up the masquerade that he was a stranger, but it broke quickly, and she lost control of it, of the mask, which kept all the grief inside. Although she was too emotional to notice, Marc's face flushed over in sadness, and a few tears fell rapidly down the cheek farthest away from her. He had liked Mary, and she would be missed, but that wasn't the whole reason. Divina's shoulders were shaking so badly, and her breaths were choppy and painful at times. Had he just walked in and found her like that, he probably would have cried a little anyway. Her sadness just blended right over into him. In all his life, he had never seen anyone so sad and letting it pour out of them so fully and with such misery.

The sound of her sadness died down a little, and she wiped her eyes, sat up just a few more inches. Staring straight ahead, she said, "You know, you should probably get away from me."

"I'm not going anywhere," Marc said.

"Just be warned. People who stay close to me tend to die."

He leaned his head over, so the sides of their heads rested on one another, ear to ear, both staring ahead.

"You know it, but I am going to say it anyway," he said. "She was very old, and it was her time to go. She lived a full life and loved you." Divina started to shake again. He kept going, the words soothing her but bringing out more mourning. "They said there wasn't any pain. She fell asleep, and it was peaceful. Imagine how happy she is wherever she happens to be now," he said. "She's looking down on you and knows you'll be okay. She knows how much you loved her, how you would have done anything to keep her here as long as possible."

"She knows that as a fact," Divina said, more to herself than to him, referring to her marriage, but Marc didn't know that.

"Her pain is over. She lived a good life, and I know I didn't know her as well as you did, but I believe that because of her stories. Anyone with stories like that..."

"She did tell one helluva a story," Divina added.

Silence fell over them. The pain was physical as if the entire body had suffered one large bruise as a whole. Mary had been holding out to see the house, and she did it. She had to let go sometime.

* * * * *

Rebecca followed the rules by the letter while she was pregnant. The last few weeks she stayed completely bedridden. If she dared even think a solitary thought of doing something out of the ordinary, of taking a walk when she should have been resting, of eating an apple when the letters said for her to have an orange, then Mr. Hamilton would fly in to the rescue and bring her back to her senses. The days had imperative rituals with the right foods, the right exercise, and the right amount of rest. She couldn't take one step more on a walk than what distance she was directed. Mr. Hamilton had Belinda making all of her food in perfect proportions and making sure Rebecca ate all of it.

Work was crushing Mr. Hamilton's time with his wife. She needed to be taken care of, and there were people here and there who already lived in the house or were hired, but he wanted to be there personally. There was no room in his mind for him not to be completely involved, making sure everything was done to code, making sure she was all right. The farm suffered slightly, but after being run for so many years, it still functioned decently. He told himself he'd make up any losses next year. The days began to consist of Rebecca, work, and sleep. After a while, this became too much. Something needed to go. He decided to sacrifice the luxury of sleep.

Work took his time during the lit hours of the day, and when night fell, he would come to Rebecca's bedside. Sometimes he'd get there early enough to see the children with her. Edgar was too young to know how to read well, so he just pretended to read and told her stories based on the pictures in the books. He made it look like he was reading the whole time. Rebecca pretended to believe him. Mr. Hamilton would stand in the doorway or on the other side of her bed from their children. Rebecca smiled often when Mr. Hamilton came in, but never with the same amount of joy as when she was in the presence of her children.

Divina brushed her mother's hair, ran small errands around the house. The little girl picked flowers and placed them around the room, opened the windows to let the surrounding darkness out of the air. She had seen her mother like this before, not while she was pregnant with Edgar, but while she was sick. Rebecca had been sick like this before, and she had gotten better. They all believed that this was just another down on the roller coaster ride of her illness, and she would ultimately come up again.

Mr. Hamilton stayed up all night at Rebecca's bedside despite how many times she told him to get some sleep, despite how many times she told him to leave because he looked so worn. He never reminded her that he had looked this worn from the beginning of her sickness. It was best to let her think it was the sleep that robbed him of his spirit.

Rebecca rested all the time, but she rarely slept. The pain was intolerable and every position uncomfortable. Talking to her husband made the days go by, the hours begin to melt. Her voice noticeably weakened every day, but her color stayed true and her hopes high. When in the height of conversation, Mr. Hamilton could almost swear that she wasn't sick at all.

On a mundane afternoon when Mr. Hamilton was out working, Belinda came into Rebecca's room with a surprised look on her face.

Stopping a board game she was playing with Edgar and Divina, Rebecca looked peacefully at her sister. "What is it, Belinda?"

"Kids, why don't you go up to your rooms," Belinda said to the children, who sat still as statues.

"Why," Divina asked, her eyebrows scrunching as if whatever it was didn't warrant an intrusion.

"It's okay, go on up," Rebecca said to them.

The children followed their mother's words obediently out of the room.

"There is someone here to see you," Belinda said with a flat voice, one harboring disrespect.

"A doctor," Rebecca asked, and then said to herself, "Was there a doctor coming today?"

"I doubt it," Belinda said sharply, turning around and beginning to walk out of the room to fetch the visitor. "Says his name is Claude. I'll send him in." Before Rebecca could retrieve her jaw from the floor, Belinda was long gone, going to fetch the guest. Claude wasn't exactly a common name, but maybe it was a doctor, maybe a coincidence...

When the silhouette entered the doorframe, she knew it was no coincidence.

Chapter 15

By the time Divina had shakily left Marc and ventured back out into the daylight, John had combed the entire farm searching for her. She found him first, hearing his anger through the rustling of the trees.

"I'll make the arrangements," John said sternly, full of strength like steel.

"I've made the arrangements, like I've already said," Edgar replied with a grown man's growl.

"I'm sorry for your loss," John said through clenched teeth. "It would be better for all of us if you just let me do this."

"Listen," Edgar said, taking a step closer to John, very close to him actually. "She was my family, not yours. I know what she wanted, and I took care of it. It's done. You try to mess with it, and--"

"You'll what? Come on, give me a real threat, Boy. I know you're grieving, so just let me take care of--"

"It's already been taken care of," Divina said, stepping in beside her brother. "Stay out of it, John."

"I've been looking for you everywhere," John said, completely forgetting about the present conversation. His voice was coated with sugar.

"I needed to be alone."

"I'm so sorry. You know I didn't mean it. Whatever you want, just ask," he said, his stance as if he was almost afraid of her, this thin woman before him with rage in her eyes and sorrow in her heart.

"The arrangements are made," Divina said with confidence, putting her hand on her brother's nearest shoulder and giving him a comforting squeeze. It was a statement, and it made John know not to say another word about it. He merely nodded.

John knew that he didn't want to be the outlet on which she got out her pain. The mourning was written all over her face, in the position of her arms. She was done being polite, the dutiful wife, the loving glue that irons out all the fights before they begin by walking away. That brittle part of her was broken in half now. John had been chewing on her last nerve, and this morning, he had bitten through. The patience was gone.

"Everything is done," Edgar said for only his sister. "You don't have to worry about anything."

"Thanks. What are you going to do now," she asked him, extremely grateful for his caring.

"I'm just going to go," he said, motioning to his apartment at the end of the house. She nodded; she understood. He had been too busy to feel the rush of emotion, but now it was coming over him like a crashing wave. Edgar was going to stretch out, in silence with only himself for company in a room. Being an old professional in grieving didn't make it any easier, but he had a system all worked out from past experience.

Divina watched him walk away, knowing he would lock the door behind him, maybe play some classical music from their mother, and remember why he hated that music with such ferocity. He might cry, he might break things, he might sit with his eyes closed and think of Mary. He'd stay there for a day, maybe more, completely isolated.

When he would resurface, no one would be able to tell he was thrashing through a pit and trying to climb out on the other side stronger. Divina would know only because she knew him. Edgar truly mourned alone.

"Do you need anything," John asked her, breaking her frame of mind away from her younger brother. He came close, put his hands on her upper arms. Reflexes were razor sharp still, and she spun inches out of his grasp. His touch was not welcome. Right now, no one's was.

"I just need to be alone," she said, walking away from him and the house. He took a few steps after her, and she didn't even turn around. "Don't follow me," she said, the direction of her voice away from him but filling his ears all the same.

Stopping cold, John knew all he could do was watch her. His tongue had spoken too fast, and she knew he loved her, but they both knew that right now, it was no consolation.

The small indent of the path back into the woods was plain as day for Divina to see. She needed to walk, and so she walked until she found herself deep within the trees, far away from human voices and human sympathy. The old house came upon her fast and without warning. She had no idea how she had walked so far in what seemed like seconds. Skipping every other step, she jumped up the staircase and entered the house.

The beauty of it even now took her breath away, and when she remembered she needed to breathe, the air was loud entering her and choking.

Mary's old room called. The space was small and lived in with a thin paisley carpet of red, navy, and crème. Her single bed still had Mary's old red comforter, hand made with goose down. Most of the dressers were empty, the closet barren. Divina shut the crème lace curtain to kill the strip of light. Pictures sat atop the nightstand along with an antique red glass lamp.

Staring at herself as a child in a yellow skirt that graced the top of her bare feet and a white shirt Belinda had sewn by hand, the picture was one of Mary's favorites. Divina's hair was cut short that summer, near the skin of her scalp, and a few pieces were longer than the others, spiky and playful. It was the look on her face that Mary had loved, the snap of the photograph taken at the exact time of the deepest part of heavy laughter. When she stared hard enough, Mary used to swear she could see the dirt under Divina's fingernails.

Divina crawled into Mary's bed, under the comforter that was so warm in the winter. The children used to do this often; it was the only place they agreed to take their naps. Mary would pull the comforter up over their heads, then back down to right under their chins. She remembered Edgar squirming and kicking in the softness of the blankets before snapping off into dream. Now, Divina rested there alone, her eyes wide open, and her feet reaching all the way to the foot of the bed.

Even the smell was the same. The scent of Mary remained in the comforter, the light honey scent of her skin which one would not have noticed unless they knew her well.

As Divina lay there alone, she realized something. She was doing exactly what her brother was doing, going off and being alone. She found a small amount of solace in that, in knowing they did this the same way. But it was frightening, being there alone, knowing Mary was truly gone. Had she said all the things she needed to say? Did they do everything they could have done? When was the last time she told Mary that she loved her?

Alone in the darkness, Divina went over these questions, and alone, she found that there was no need to be afraid of her sadness. There was something powerful there, something that said because she didn't need anyone right now, then no one would let her down. In these first hours, she was sure that if she became vulnerable, and John said the wrong thing, then it may be intolerable. It may be impossible to fix. Divina knew people have to do this on their own, but mostly, they have someone to hold them or call if they need anything, but she needed physical separation as well as emotional. Only when some strength returned, then she could go back and handle the pity, the cards, the feelings no one knew quite how to say in words.

Dusk settled outside the window. The light she had been keeping out with the curtains was gone now. Divina stretched her legs under the covers, and she slowly made her way to sitting up. Placing her feet on the floor, she remembered sitting here as a child when her legs were so short that her feet didn't reach. She remembered jumping down when now all she had to do was stand. The moonlight was calling. With a few brief steps, she reached the window, and pulled the curtains back.

The energy from merely walking drained from her limbs. Divina crawled back into bed, leaving the windows open, the air blowing in the room. Stars glittered from where she slept, and the moon's reflection was present at the top of the window. The sky was her night-light.

The choice was barely conscious. Divina spent the night in the house, in her home.

John knew where she was, but he didn't dare interrupt her. The night was long, and he waited for her to come back and sleep. When she didn't and morning came, he wondered if she ever would.

* * * * *

"What are you doing here," Rebecca asked. Her eyes were as wide as saucers. With a sudden gust of energy, she sat up in bed.

"I came to see how you're doing."

Claude's blond hair was messy and ragged as if he had been traveling for months. He wore faded blue jeans and a gray tee shirt. His shadow was strange touching the floors of this house.

This was the first time he was entering a house in which she lived. Through everything, she had always walked through his door even when she lived with him. Now, he had finally walked through hers.

"My husband--"

"He's working. I checked. Give me some credit, Rebecca."

"He doesn't know you exist."

Claude took this in. He had assumed it but never heard it out loud. She knew from the look on his face that it stung. She had been lying to her husband all the times she had gone to New York. Claude had figured this, and yet now he knew he had never believed she could do it, the lying, the sneaking away.

"Not that he has any reason to worry. You chose him over me before you met him," Claude said ruefully.

"Stop it," she said harshly. "You didn't come here for this."

"Sorry."

"You must really think I am about to die."

"I wanted to hear from you why you haven't come back."

Rebecca realized he didn't know. He couldn't even tell standing right in front of her. The blankets were thick and the comforter deep, wrinkled. Claude didn't see the bulge of her stomach. He had no idea she was pregnant, only that she was sick again.

Her maternal instinct came in immediately, the loyalty obvious and concrete. "I haven't been well, but I'll get better in a few months. Then, we'll see each other again."

He came closer, put his hand on her forehead.

Rebecca saw the wisp of hair a few feet above the floor in the doorway. "Damn," she whispered.

Claude thought she had felt a stab of pain.

"Come here, Honey," Rebecca said.

Claude turned to see the young girl at the door, porcelain skinned like her mother with the same blue eyes.

"Hi," Divina said to him.

"Hi," Claude replied, and then he reached down, offering his hand.

Divina shook it with a politeness taught from birth.

"This is my daughter, Divina," Rebecca said to him.

"Nice to meet you," he said to the little girl.

"Who are you," Divina asked him, her tiny lips smiling. She liked this man because her mother had that soft expression on her face although she didn't look particularly happy.

Claude didn't have a chance to answer.

"Someone who helped me with my sketches when I was younger," Rebecca answered. "Why don't you go and see if Belinda can make me something to eat. I'm starving."

Divina's face lit up. Her mother was hungry! Her mother was never hungry. She darted out of the room like a rabbit. She knew very well that her mother should be eating. Eating would make her healthy again.

"See," Rebecca said to Claude. "My children need me right now. When I feel better and have some time, we'll see each other."

"Promise," he asked her.

"Promise."

"Is there anything you want? I can stay for a few days, come around when it's appropriate."

"No," she said quickly, decisively. "I think you should go."

Claude put his hands in his pockets and lowered his head, so his hair fell over his eyebrows. He looked around, silent for a few seconds. His eyes rested on it immediately. His stare didn't leave it.

"Sadly, that makes me very happy," he said as he studied it. It was on the wall she stared at from her bed, high enough for her perfect view, the painting he had made of her.

"You know I always loved that painting," she said.

"You didn't even know what it was at first," he scolded with a soft voice, finding the humor in her words.

"Doesn't matter. I loved it then, and I love it now." He was quiet, peaceful standing there in her room. "You know," she said seriously, "I'm okay."

"I just wanted to see, know for sure."

"I understand." Her voice quieted to barely above a whisper. "It was good to see you."

Claude leaned over and kissed her forehead, the kiss lingering longer than normal kisses given on foreheads. "I should go then, let you rest."

She reached out and squeezed his hand, letting it go with just as much speed. "Goodbye," she said without sadness as if she saw him every day.

"Bye," he said, and smiled at her, his eyes so blue and lucid. "I'll see you in a few months then."

She watched him begin to walk out of the room, his stride slow and purposeful, riddled with deep thoughts of things he should say.

His feet were still pointing toward the door when he stopped, and he turned his body just enough to look at her again. "Sometimes, I miss you, you know?"

"Yeah, I miss you, too," she said, forcing herself to make the words clear and concise and intelligent.

With that he was gone, and although she knew, he had no idea. The tears were quiet. Her body didn't move with them. They landed on her lips, and she tasted them, her sweetness, her sadness.

Claude would see her again. She had not lied to him.

But this would be the last time she would be able to say goodbye to him.

* * * * *

Divina crept back into John's house like she was a thief. John found her before she woke up. She hadn't been there long, but for all he knew, she could have been there all night. She slept on the couch.

He decided not to wake her. There was work to be done. He took some papers and the portable phone into the kitchen. Divina heard him walk into the other room and start speaking, and she overheard the conversation. "Yes," John said on the phone. "I know. We've had livestock here and there, but never enough to be considered for anything."

There was a pause.

"I know. They were a gift. I need some more hands that know what they are doing in this area of expertise. Most of my employees are equipped for their present jobs in the fields and with the machinery."

Divina got up and walked closer to his voice. John had evidently made a business deal and somehow managed to not only do well in the deal but get some free cattle. Some may not be a word to give it justice. He wasn't a rancher, but now he had enough cattle to call the farm a ranch.

"Great. Sounds wonderful. I'll talk to you again tomorrow," John said as he hung up the phone. He felt her eyes on him before he turned to see her.

"Livestock?"

"Good morning. How are you doing," he asked her with sympathy.

"How much livestock?"

"You remember that deal with--"

"What kind of livestock?"

John drew in a breath. "We have a couple more cows coming."

"Define a couple."

"Okay, we have quite a few cows coming, but hear me out."

Divina sat across from John at the kitchen table. It was the first time she took the place that wasn't beside him. She sat across from him as his equal now, and just sitting there gave her more power.

Neither her face nor her words showed anger. There was a serenity about her, but it harbored on dangerous as if she would break into a rage at any moment.

"They were a gift," John said.

"So I heard."

"We definitely have the room, and we can hire a couple more people. It will make us a ton of money," he said.

"I always liked cows," she said to herself although her eyes showed frustration.

"And Claude might like them. He really likes the few animals we have now. They're more interesting to him than any plants out in the fields," John said as if Claude had been his entire motivation for the whole thing.

"I was really good with livestock when we had them once in a while on the farm," she said, referring to her childhood.

"That's right," John said, remembering.

"Good, then I can do this."

"Do what?"

"You've got yourself a worker," she said.

"That's ridiculous," he said, not thinking she was serious.

"That," she said as she got up from the table, "is not negotiable."

"Why? Just tell me why."

She stopped on her way out of the room. "Because I can't sit here in this house. I have to do something, John. You know damn well you couldn't live the way you expect me to live."

"That's different."

"Bullshit!"

"Fine, you're grieving. You need something to take your mind off--"

"Don't put this into some strange mourning category."

"Why don't you join a club or something?"

"I want to work, something I can sink my fingers into. Do you honestly see me handing out programs for some organization?"

"Sorry. It's fine. Do it then. If it makes you happy," he began, but he didn't get to finish the sentence.

Divina had heard what she had wanted to hear, and beyond that, she had heard enough. She had one last thing to add to the conversation, so before John could evaluate what had just been said, she shouted back towards the kitchen. "And Edgar and Marc are going to be working with me!"

Divina didn't wait for an answer.

Within the week, the livestock arrived. There were more then anyone had imagined. This was going to be quite a project. John knew he should never have agreed to this. He wondered if he'd ever see his wife again. He didn't care about Edgar or Marc. They were good workers but nothing spectacular to his business. Divina also had told him that Marc had a lot of prior experience with livestock. John wasn't sure whether to question Divina's belief in Marc's stories, but he decided it was best to let her be loyal.

He didn't want to get into another pointless battle with her where no one wins. Stepping out of an older building where some of the cows were being placed, John didn't recognize her right away. Clad in old rags, older than perhaps even his years on earth, Divina's face had smudged dirt crossing her features. The most dramatic part was her hair.

She had taken the gut instinct and done it herself. Tired of it and of waiting for it to dry and of babying it, she took the small kitchen scissors and chopped it away. The length was gone, the body gone, and what was left was a messy and easy cut.

Divina knew had she mentioned it to John, he would have forbidden it. The cut was not one of an important wife. He wondered if that was precisely why she had done it. Inside, she told herself it had nothing to do with John. She couldn't have long hair and work as hard as she wanted. She didn't want the time or the inconvenience of it. But a part of her did find pleasure from the fact that John would never approve of it.

John walked away, shook hands with those who delivered the animals, and went back to business. It would grow back, he told himself. Let it go. She's grieving. People do insane things when they grieve.

Over the noise of the cows and conversations, Edgar's voice was loud and clear. "I like your hair," he yelled to Divina.

"Thanks," she responded, her voice sounding almost happy.

"It's almost shorter than mine," Marc said jokingly.

She made a scowling face at him sarcastically.

The fences and buildings were perfect for the animals. The cows were of all shades of browns and blacks, young and old, with big eyes. For the most part, they were wild, but Divina, Edgar, and Marc knew how to handle themselves instantly. There were no unseen disturbances, and they spoke calmly, the cows and their nerves from traveling wore down and relaxed as if this was a normal day with ritual occurrences.

As the trucks pulled away, Divina knew John had gone back to his work somewhere far from wherever she was. She put it to the back of her mind. The workers sorted the cows, decided which pastures and buildings would go with which bunches. The animals were hosed off and fed and checked by vets who said they were in fits of health. As evening appeared in a dark blue wave, Edgar, Marc, and Divina found their fellow workers thinning out.

"You really are going to be attached, aren't you," Marc asked Divina with a loud laugh.

She was playing with a few of the calves, the smallest one following her around. Their coats were soft and gentle and their bodies so warm. They were so very alive and sweet. "Probably," she said honestly.

"Happens every time," Edgar said to Marc.

"You guys can go. We're pretty much done for the day," she said.

"Okay. Good night," Edgar replied, and he began to kick his boots against the side of the nearest fence, shaking off the excess muck and mud. He turned and disappeared rapidly.

Divina knew he was tired by the way he walked, trying so hard to keep up the proud exterior, when on the inside, his joints were screaming. She could recognize it a hundred feet away.

Marc petted the white star on a little black calf who walked up to him as he sat on a bucket turned upside down. "Are you going to stay here a while?"

"Yeah," she said, running a few steps and then quickly changing her direction as a few calves tried to clumsily keep up with her.

"Can I stay?"

"You don't have to worry about me. I'm fine. I'm sad, of course, but I'm fine," she said to Marc.

"I know. I'm sad, too, but I'm not worried. I'd just like to hang out a little, let the breeze relax me, you know?"

"Yeah," she said, stopping in her tracks and reaching out for one of the calves.

The breeze was strong and welcome, like ice water when you feel as if you haven't had a drink in days, like a shadow when you've been in the sweltering sun for hours.

"I don't want to admit it, but…" he began, embarrassed.

"I know," she said, seeing what he was going to say. "They're damn cute."

Then, they both laughed at themselves. It felt good, the laughter. The stars came out winking at them long before they retreated from the day.

The first few days were the hardest, figuring out what to do and how long it would take to get everything done. After a while, they got the hang of it. They learned which groups of cows took longer, had tempers, and which were as easy as snapping fingers. The work didn't compel the mind, but it took up the day and time and swallowed up a lot of effort. The day began at sunrise, when the air was still littered with a small bit of chill, and then it was half finished by the time midday heat made an appearance. The last part of the day occurred around suppertime, which was convenient because Divina didn't have to cook or eat with anyone. She grabbed a sandwich on the run or ate earlier in the day before John came home.

She was liking her marriage more and more.

By the time John fell asleep waiting up, she slipped in as evasive as a ghost in the house. Edgar would leave just before the sun went down, when the horizon was a watercolor painting of reds and oranges and pinks. Marc stuck around longer, finishing up details with Divina, talking to her, and admiring the playfulness of the calves long into the evening.

Their conversations could be polite and boring, or sometimes, they were deep and prolific. On a night about a month after the cattle had been delivered, they had a conversation while sitting on a gate on the outside of one of the main barns, overlooking the fields and the remaining light over the land. The cows were quiet expect for an occasional cry, but mostly, the insects and birds were the only song in the air.

"I realized something today," Divina said to Marc. "While Edgar and I were feeding the calves."

"What did you realize?"

"That you're my friend. I realized that when you came right over when that cow nearby was going to get out of the pen, and you jumped right in front of me."

"You just figured that out? Where have you been the last couple years?"

"I know, I know, but you're Edgar's friend." Her cheeks turned red. She felt silly.

"You can have the same friends as your brother. You knew that before."

"Not really. I've never really..."

"What? Never what? Been friends with someone who was friends with your brother? That's understandable. He's always been a lot younger than you."

144

"No, it's just... I've never really had a friend before. Besides John."

"Seriously?"

"John's the only one who lived around here. School was on and off, and then when my parents died, it was just relatives around."

"That's sad. I don't think I would have survived without friends."

"I know, I sound silly and ungrateful. I don't mean that. I had lots of people in my life... Never mind. I guess I am just rattling on," she said, wondering what had possessed her to say that to him.

"No, I mean, I am really honored," Marc said, his face opening into a smile. He put his arm around her shoulder and gave her a small hug. "It's good for the ego."

"Oh, here goes. I've created a monster," she yelled, shrieking back in laughter.

They both laughed some more, and the conversation became lighter. As they parted for the night, Marc had been trying to think of what to say. No one had ever looked at him with such sincerity before tonight.

Just before they left, he said his piece quickly, and at the end, he took her smile as her response, and they parted with his words as the last they shared. "You know," he said, "you and Edgar are really important to me, too. I don't have any family here. You two are the ones that make up my life here. I don't know what I would do if you weren't around. I probably would have left a long time ago."

Chapter 16

"Here's your food," Belinda said hastily, setting the tray down loudly next to Rebecca.

"Belinda," Rebecca began.

"What? It's none of my business who the strange man was." Belinda waited a moment then couldn't control herself any longer. "Who was he?"

"An old friend."

"Smart guy, sneaking in here when your husband isn't around to catch him. That's not suspicious or anything."

"Listen, Belin--"

"I know you're not that stupid. You're just not. Your marriage is good, practically one of the best I've ever seen. You truly love each other."

"You're not telling me anything I don't know."

"He's from New York--" Belinda began to ask.

"He's from before I had set foot in Louisiana."

"Then, why was he here? Never mind, don't answer that. I don't want to hear you say it," she barked.

"Do you honestly think--"

"Don't patronize me, Little Sister. Just promise me one thing."

"What?"

"Tell me he's not coming back into this house. Ever."

"Belinda, I'll have whoever I want in this house--"

"Promise me, or I'll--"

"You'll what," Rebecca snapped.

"I'll ask your husband about our guest."

The look on Rebecca's face told Belinda that she had guessed right. Mr. Hamilton didn't know a man from New York existed in Rebecca's life. "Do you want to hurt me," Rebecca asked with surprise.

"Of course not. If it were just you and your husband, I wouldn't give a damn. I wouldn't approve, but I wouldn't necessarily care either."

"You don't know the whole situation."

"As I was saying," Belinda continued while looking at her sister who wanted to speak, too. "I wouldn't care. But when you start introducing your men to your *children*, that's when I have a problem."

"Good Lord, he's not one of my men. I don't have any men."

Belinda looked at her sister skeptically. "Maybe not in this room right now, but--"

"I thought you had more faith in me than that."

"I have a lot of faith in you, but you have to remember, I've known you your whole life. I know the signs. I know the cycles. You're not perfect, Rebecca. You never were."

"I love you, too," she said sarcastically.

"I know you're in pain, and you don't want to hurt anyone--"

"Of course, I don't want to hurt anyone!"

"Rebecca, calm down. You'll work yourself up into a tizzy. Maybe these men alleviate some of your pain. And if no one knows, then great for you. But if your family finds out, then everyone is going to hurt just as much as you."

"I don't have men. Claude was it. Just let me explain, Belinda. Please." The look in her eyes was deep, sad, pleading.

Belinda let out a large sigh, not really wanting to hear it. But she walked over and locked the door to the bedroom then took a seat next to Rebecca. "Go ahead. I'm listening."

"Don't look at me like that," Rebecca said with hurt in her voice. "I'm not going to tell you what you think you're going to hear."

"We'll see."

"I haven't been seeing Claude during the duration of my marriage."

Belinda rolled her eyes. "Then, who have you been seeing?"

"Wait, I didn't mean that. I mean, I've been seeing Claude--" Belinda scoffed. Rebecca shot her a scowl. "For years. He's my best friend, and he's been there. But I haven't been running off and cheating on my husband since my honeymoon."

"Were you and Claude ever involved before this?"

Rebecca waited a moment to answer. She knew how her sister would take this. "He was the one in New York, Belinda. The one I stayed in New York for when Dad thought I was coming back."

Belinda's eyebrows shot up her forehead. Of all the men Rebecca had seen and spoken of and lived with in her lifetime, there was only one that

Belinda remembered. That was the one.

Rebecca had really loved him. She stayed away from her family and nearly was disowned because of him. For many years, she lived with that man in New York. Belinda could have kicked herself for not figuring it out sooner. He was from New York. The connection was obvious.

Belinda ran her hand over her own forehead, feeling the warmth of the stress level inside of her rising. "Tell me the story," she said, and then quickly added with a deep and serious tone, "All of it. Tell me all of it."

Belinda sat mostly motionless except for an occasional nod of the head or pat on her sister's hand. Rebecca told her the whole story, from the beginning when she first met Claude on the roof to the last goodbye, which happened a few hours earlier.

For once, instead of judging, Belinda hugged her sister. The understanding was mutual.

* * * * *

"I have a surprise for you," Marc said to Divina as they finished closing up one of the barns.

"Seriously? A good surprise or a bad surprise?"

He laughed. "Always so negative. A good surprise, of course."

She clapped her hands together with a mix of fake and real enthusiasm.

They had been working together for half a year now with the cattle. Mary's death was still a wound, but it wasn't as fresh and didn't sting as much. Edgar and Divina were handling it well, often saying it must be because they've had so much practice. The cattle were doing well, not terrific, but not terrible.

Just like her father, Divina said, "Next year, we'll blow everyone else away. Next year, that will be the year we reap all the benefits."

She had that same drive and determination. Edgar nodded in agreement, not daring to question his sister.

"I'll give it to you after we get done working," Marc said to Divina.

"You're so mean, getting me all curious and then making me wait."

"That's the plan," he said with a grin.

With the promise of something new and exciting, the rest of the work dragged on and on. Finally, they finished everything, and Marc lingered as he always did at the end of the day.

148

"No way," Divina said, pushing him up before he could sit all the way down on a square bale of hay.

"Whatever could you mean?"

"Gift," she said with her eyes shining.

"Oh yeah, I almost forgot. Are you saying you'd rather skip our normal witty conversation and just leave for the day?"

"Yes," she said seriously. He knew she would. She followed Marc around the corner to the small office where he did paperwork. It wasn't nice or large; it was located in the front of one of the barns. He walked in and took out a large, flat thing wrapped in brown paper.

"Open it," he said, handing the package to her.

She tore it open like a child at Christmas, and upon seeing it, she stopped cold. Her eyes froze and her arms stopped moving. It was the painting.

"Thank you," she said, then ran over and, still holding the large painting in one hand, gave him a big hug.

The affection surprised him, but he automatically returned her gesture.

"Are you going to hang it in your living room," he asked.

"No, I'm hanging it in my bedroom where it belongs." Upon seeing his flicker of reaction, she quickly added, "In the old house, in the bedroom where I grew up."

"But you'll never see it," he said.

"It'll give me an excuse to go check the old house. Besides, I don't think I'd like it in that house."

"Why?"

"I don't really know. When I figure it out, I'll give you a call," she said, confused herself. Then, she leaned up, very quickly and bird like, and gave him a kiss on the cheek.

If the hug surprised him, then the polite kiss shocked him. But as she walked out of his office to head over to the old house, no one was more stunned than she was.

Walking down the path in the trees, she wondered what had possessed her to do that. Sure, Marc was a good friend, but she had never been one of those women who physically touched others in gestures during conversations. Divina realized it had been months since she had been given a hug. She missed the human contact. John was still angry with her, and sometimes she didn't even know why. There was no way she was going to ask. Things always got worse when she stood up for herself and gave him reasons why

149

she did the things that angered him. She chalked up giving Marc a hug to loneliness. He knew her well and was as close to her as anyone had ever been, and she knew he wouldn't take it to heart or make a big deal out of it.

When Divina returned after hanging up the picture, she saw the lights on. John was waiting for her. She tried to summon energy. This was going to be a long night. For the life of her, she couldn't think of what she had done this time.

John sat at the kitchen table, his honorary seat, his throne over which he ruled his domain. Divina took the seat opposite of him. She had since Mary died, never returning to the seat next to him.

It wasn't that she hadn't tried to fix things. She apologized to him time and again for acting how she did after Mary's death, but no, that didn't mean she was going to stop working. No, that didn't mean she was going to let her hair grow back. That wasn't the point. She worked it out, so that she started work later and could eat with John in the evenings. She left notes for him, sometimes with a message related to work, other times just to say good morning. But they had not clicked again. The jagged pieces which used to be tolerable refused to go back into place with any degree of comfort.

"What are you doing up," she asked him. She placed her arms on the table, making herself appear to take up more room than she really did.

"Waiting for you."

"Did something happen? Is Claude..."

"No, nothing happened. To the best of my knowledge, he's fine."

She waited, racking her brain on what she may have done or said which offended him.

"Can I ask you something?"

"Sure," she replied cautiously.

"What happened to us?" For the first time, she had no idea how to respond. "It was so good in the beginning."

"Things change," she said.

"No kidding. You're certainly not the woman I married." His words held no anger or bitterness, but that didn't stop the sting. John had a tendency to say things and not consider how they sounded, how they would wound.

"What's that suppose to mean? I certainly am the same," she said. She thought about it, and knew although she was sure she had changed in small ways, she had basically stayed the same. She was strong, determined,

150

opinionated. He knew when he married her that she wasn't going to be a stay at home wife. He knew her. "Why did you marry me?"

"Where did that come from," she asked as her voice got higher and higher.

"Was it for money?"

"John!" She knew her face was betraying her mask of strength. The hurt was running all over it. "How could you even say that? How could you!"

"Truthfully, Divina. Tell me the truth. You weren't in love with me."

"I didn't marry you for money. There. Are you happy now? Is that what you were waiting to hear? The words? Because I know inside that you can't possibly believe that. You can't."

"Then, why did you marry me?"

Divina knew she had to pick her words carefully. He was obviously already hurt, thinking up a scheming scenario in his mind. They hadn't had a romantic courtship; they both knew that. "John, you took care of me so much--" she began.

"You knew I would always take care of you. No matter what."

"That's not the point. I knew that. But I couldn't let it be that way anymore."

"So, basically, you thought you'd pay me back by marrying me?"

"You make me sound like a prostitute. That's not it at all."

"Then, what is it?"

"It was time for us to start taking care of each other, John." He waited in silence. "Can you understand that," she asked him, getting up and walking over to him, leaving her high post at the other end of the table. She reached him and was about to put her arms around him, but he was too proud.

He didn't hear what she had said. "So, you're telling me you never loved me."

"John--" she started.

He had known it, but he had expected her to lie. Somehow, he had wanted her to lie. Pushing back his chair and getting up on the other side of it, he moved away from her. She took one step toward him, and he put up a hand. Don't follow me is what his gesture said. Then, he walked out of the room. He had heard all he wanted to hear.

She sat down in his chair, unsure what to do. Wondering what things would have been like took over her thoughts. What if she had started having children from the beginning, stayed home and raised them? Would things be different? Would she love him? Would she be happy?

Somewhere inside her private thoughts, she knew although children would probably have changed her, she still felt like a child. She knew that she would have loved them and done her best. Remembering her mother, she also knew it wouldn't have been enough. She would have to have some other outlet, some place to go other than another room in the house. There was something deeper inside her that told her the life she had chosen to lead was not going to be enough to fulfill her days and bring her any sort of happiness.

If she had learned anything throughout this life, it was that you couldn't wait in case happiness someday arrived. You had to go after it, find it, and latch onto it. Because you never know when today is your last day, and there will be no tomorrow for you.

* * * * *

Rebecca saw Divina's innocent eyes staring at her, holding the wet rag to her forehead. The last contraction had been worse than all the others before. Rebecca refused to let out a sound. Not in front of her daughter.

"Don't be scared," Rebecca said to her.

"I'm not, Mom."

Rebecca smiled weakly. The little girl didn't know what she should be afraid of. The pain subsided before, and she believed with all her soul that it would subside again. There just was no other option.

"Why don't you go and put some fresh water on that rag, Honey."

"Okay, Mom."

"Divina?"

"Yes," the little voice said before she turned to leave.

"I love you."

Divina jumped up and kissed her mother on the cheek. She had such energy. "I love you, too, Mom. I'll be right back."

Rebecca knew it wouldn't be long now. She could feel it. The pain was intense and bone splitting, but she stayed awake throughout.

Rebecca knew Divina had not come back into the room many more times. She was unsure whether her husband stayed the whole time or whether he left the room periodically. Faces and voices were blurry, strangely unfamiliar.

She knew she should be terrified, but she had other things on her mind.

Waiting and trying, finally nearly fainting from exhaustion, it happened.

Rebecca heard her baby crying. She had been fighting and fighting, but she just couldn't hold on anymore.

She was gone.

Chapter 17

Divina laid down on the couch. She didn't dare to be in the same room with John. Fighting took the energy out of her, but it also made her angry, which fueled a certain passion inside.

When John woke to go to work in the morning, and he walked down the hall, there was no missing her. She was sitting up straight in the dim shadows of the morning. He nearly screamed; she had surprised him so much. "I'm not doing this anymore," she said through the darkness.

"Have you been sitting there all night?"

"You have to pick right now."

"Pick between what," John asked, confused.

"Because I can't live like this anymore. Every time you look at me, you glare at me like I broke some kind of deal. The thing is, I never knew there was a deal."

"I do not."

"It's up to you, John, because I am not going to feel like I've done something terrible any more. I'm not going to be mad at myself for not being whoever it is you wanted me to be."

"You're exactly who I want you to be."

"You pick, John. We can work this thing out, or you can ask for a divorce. I don't want anything for a settlement. It's simple. No strings."

"Who said anything about a divorce? I didn't."

"You never said anything about staying married either."

"Did you really take our vows that lightly? Did it mean nothing to you?"

"Yeah, John, that's it exactly. I thought it would be fun to get married and divorced," she said with bitter sarcasm. "I am not going to try if I am the only one. I can't fix this. Stop expecting me to."

"Sure you can. It's all in your hands," he lectured.

"How? By going barefoot and having a couple kids? Joining the gardener's club in town? Would that fix things?"

"Yes. It would be a start."

"The thing is," she said, lowering her voice, "I don't want to do those things. I never have, and I probably never will."

He was taken aback.

"The way I am, the way I've always been, is going to be the way that I am next year, ten years from now, and probably fifty years from now. Either you're going to have to get over this idea of me that you had when we got married, of whoever it was I was going to instantly transform into."

"I accept you as you are. You know that."

"No, you don't. You would if I changed, but I am not going to change. So, you can find someone more suited for you. I hear there are women who want to be wives. Even when we were children, did you ever honestly expect me to get married and just stop--"

"No--"

"Stop working, stop taking care of Claude and Edgar, stop setting goals, stop reaching for things that maybe I shouldn't be reaching for?"

"No. I love that about you."

"Then stop acting like it's a crime when I want to work, when I want to be by myself."

"I'm sorry, but you and I are supposed to be living a life together, not two completely separate ones."

"Well, I can't do that. I need my own life. I can't be an extension of yours. Maybe you can't handle that. We probably should have never gotten married in the first place--"

"Don't ever say that. I have never regretted marrying you, not even for a second."

She gave him a look that said she didn't believe him. After all, she had definitely had moments when she wished she had never married, never moved out of the old house, never changed her entire life.

"As long as I live, I will never allow us to dissolve our marriage. We're in this for the long haul. Until death, Divina. Every couple has problems--"

"Problems? You're referring to what we have as problems? You sure know how to make an understatement."

"You know I'll never leave you. You're my wife. I'll do whatever it takes. We'll work on this."

"If that's what you want--"

"No, that's what is going to happen. There is no choice."

"Okay," she said, her voice withering out.

155

"So, what do we do now," he asked her.

"How should I know?"

* * * * *

Mr. Hamilton died shortly after Rebecca. The time was actually short enough that they held one funeral for the both of them. It was easier on everyone involved.

Claude slipped in the back of the old church and sat in the last pew on the end. He sat through the entire service, quiet and unnoticed. The people began to thin out afterwards, most had come early to give their best wishes and sympathy. A diner down the road was where most of the group was going to eat and reminisce after.

A few individuals lingered, spread far apart around the large room. The light filtered brilliant colors on the wooden floor from the stained glass windows. Children were playing outside.

Divina and Edgar were still in the church, standing near the front, each dressed well and extremely quiet. The shock was still settling in. Belinda stood next to them, holding the baby, saying goodbye to the last of the guests.

Claude didn't even recognize them. He walked slowly up to the front. His clothes would have made her laugh; this he knew for sure. He wore a black suit, his hair cut shorter than ever before, very professional. He could have been a banker. She would have loved the image.

Belinda recognized him right away. She wanted to be angry he was here, but no matter how hard she tried, she was indifferent. He could do whatever he wanted. She didn't care.

This was the first time Claude had seen Mr. Hamilton. He merely nodded at him in respect, having no words to say because he never knew the man. Claude lingered by Rebecca, saddened seeing her like this. He tried to hold back, but his eyes filled with tears. It wasn't supposed to be like this. With all her dreams or even with his dreams, it was never suppose to be like this.

Claude reached down and touched her hand. She was so still. He couldn't say it out loud, so in his head, he let the word goodbye float through his mind.

That was when the baby started to cry, and he saw Belinda with Rebecca's little girl and what he assumed to be Rebecca's little boy. Belinda

156

looked up and saw Claude's surprise. He hadn't known there had been a baby. Belinda wondered why she wasn't surprised.

"I know that man," Divina said, her eyes red and skin blotchy. "Hey, Mister," she yelled when it seemed he was ready to disappear out the nearest door. Claude walked over as if he had been planning it all along. "You were Mom's friend," Divina said.

"Yes, I was. I'm sorry for your loss," he said to her and to the others.

"I'm sorry for your loss, too, then," Divina said politely.

"Thank you."

"We'd better be going," Belinda interjected.

"We're going to the restaurant. Do you want to come," Divina asked him.

Belinda opened and then shut her mouth again.

"No, no. I have to get back." Claude smiled at her. His eyes then rested on the baby.

"That's my little brother," Divina said. "His name is Claude. What's yours?"

Belinda stared at him. The obvious surprise ran through his body. He didn't even bother to hide his reaction when he realized that Divina was staring at him, waiting for an answer. "I have to go," he said quickly, almost rudely. He then turned and practically ran out the door.

"Come on, Kids. We have to go and eat now. A lot of people are waiting to talk to you," Belinda said, gently pushing them with her knee toward the other exit.

"Okay," Edgar said.

Divina fell into step beside her brother. "Do you think that man's going to be okay," she asked her aunt.

"I'm sure he's fine. He probably had somewhere to be. People lead busy lives when they grow up, Honey."

"Did he not like Claude? Maybe he doesn't like babies?"

"I'm sure that had nothing to do with it. Besides, look at Claude. How could anyone not fall in love with him on sight?"

Divina smiled and touched the top of Claude's bald head. The explanation seemed fitting.

* * * * *

Marc heard all about John and Divina's relationship from Divina. This week, it had been about how they were going to work things out.

"How do you suppose people go about that," she asked Marc.

"That's the whole reason I'm not married. So I don't have to think about questions like that," he replied.

"You're a big help."

"Are you trying to tell me that I don't help you? Okay, that's completely true," he said with a laugh.

She made a face at him but broke out in a smile. "Why are you so easy to talk to," she asked him.

"Because I'm amazing."

"Yes, but that doesn't explain anything."

"Should I be flattered or offended by where this is going?"

"Flattered," she said with confidence. "I can say a few sentences to you, and you completely understand what I am talking about. I can talk to John about the same thing for days on end, and he still won't see that I have a point."

"John's a... unique guy."

Divina laughed so hard she had to hold onto a nearby fence to steady herself. "I have to go," she said. "I heard from one of the workers that they saw someone around the old house yesterday. I think," she said, clapping her hands together in excitement," we may have a wanderer."

"Is that good news?"

"Absolutely! I loved when people came through when I was little. They were always so interesting. Maybe whoever it is needs a meal and will end up telling us his life story."

"You aren't going by yourself," Marc said.

"Oh, God, Marc. I can take care of myself."

"Okay, that's it. I'm going with you. End of conversation. New subject."

"Marc--"

"You aren't talking me out of this one, Divina."

She stopped talking and accepted his protective attempt. He wasn't going to change his mind. It didn't matter. They began the walk to the old house.

Marc followed Divina faithfully. She was so familiar with the woods and the path. It was almost inhuman. With one infamous turn, they were looking upon the grand home.

"We did a good job. Looks good even in the dark," he joked. He didn't see but knew she was smiling again. Her smiles were coming easier, which he took as a good sign.

There was a single light on in the upstairs. They both knew they hadn't left any lights on. Divina didn't know why, but she felt a shiver crawl up her spine. There was no silhouette, but there was a definite light. "If you repeat this, I'll deny it, but I'm glad your here," she said to Marc. He could barely hear her.

"It's a good thing I have my tape recorder on then," he responded.

She hit the back of his head lightly with her palm.

"Ow," he said, trying not to laugh.

They reached the stairs. Divina was careful not to make any noise. This was her house. If anything was missing or broken...

Marc opened the door slowly, not letting Divina go in first. They peered around the corners. There was no evidence of anyone entering before them.

They climbed the stairs, coming closer and closer to the room with the light. The door was wide open. If someone was in there, they should have been able to see him through the window from the outside.

"Let me," Divina said to Marc, her voice hushed. He didn't have the time to argue. She cowered low, and then, very slowly, stole a glance around the corner. She stood with just as much gradual motion. Her entire body was in the frame of the doorway.

"What are you doing," Marc hissed at her.

"Excuse me," she said loudly, kindly, and not to Marc.

The stranger turned around. Sitting on the floor, it was no wonder they hadn't seen anyone through the window. "I heard no one lived in this house any more. I wondered if it was for sale," the stranger said. "I couldn't get a straight answer from anyone, so I just showed up. I'm sorry if I'm intruding."

"I know you," she said, bending down right in front of him, reaching her hand out like she wanted to touch his face. Then, it came to her. She knew where she had seen him before. "I guess you don't recognize me."

His eyes searched her, then lit up when it hit him. Claude didn't know why he hadn't seen it sooner. She looked exactly like her mother. They had identical eyes.

Claude had been sitting there, staring at his painting.

"You know this guy," Marc asked with a whisper to Divina even though he was loud enough for the whole room to hear.

She cocked her head from side to side as she studied Claude. "Yes, I do. This is a friend of my mother's. Therefore, he is a friend of mine."

"Okay," Marc said, not convinced. He would have to be dragged from that spot if anyone tried to make him leave. There was no way he was leaving Divina with this guy. Something about him made Marc wonder about him. First of all, he seemed all too comfortable in this house.

"How long have you been here," she asked Claude.

"Since the day before yesterday. I was going to leave right after just looking at the place--"

"Yeah right," Marc muttered. Divina shot Marc a murderous look. He closed his mouth.

"I was going to leave, but I just wanted to stay a little longer. Seems silly, but," he said, looking at Marc, "it's the truth."

"You must be hungry. Please come and eat. I live right through the woods. We have warm food and a nice couch you can sleep on."

"Thank you. May I ask why you moved? Is there something wrong with this house? It's understandable why you might not want to be here twenty-four hours a day,' Claude said. He knew the place was full of memories.

"I wish I could be here twenty four hours a day," she said, happy with the thought. Claude looked at her, his eyes questioning. "I moved when I got married."

"Oh," he said, clear about it now.

"Please come," Divina said, stretching her legs. Claude stood with her, and they began their trip to John's house. Divina was chatting on and on, excited to be talking to someone who had known her mother well. Her mouth was racing. They walked in the door just as Divina caught herself. "You know, I never even asked you your name," she said, embarrassed. "Sometimes I just get talking and keep talking."

"Your mother used to do that exact thing," he responded, his wrinkled face soft.

"Really?" She was pleased with that remark.

Belinda was in the kitchen, trying to find some pan or another. She looked up at the voices and dropped the dish she was holding onto the floor. It shattered, silencing everyone. "Claude," she said, her voice a monotone.

He was as surprised to see her as she was him. Divina saw the look on her aunt's face and took a few steps back from the stranger. There was fear in Belinda's eyes. That was nothing to be taken lightly. "I'm sorry," Claude said, backing up, retreating from the center of the room.

"There is nothing for you here," Belinda said without anger but with force.

"Of course, it was never my intention," he said earnestly. Claude disappeared out the door almost as quickly as Divina had found him.

Belinda knew from the look on Divina's face that there was no way to escape an explanation. Her eyes were wide as saucers. The little girl she remembered was gone now, gone since the marriage, but reappearing briefly here and there. At this moment, there might as well have been no little girl in the past.

"What was that," Divina asked.

"It was something from a long time ago--"

"I hope it was an important 'something' because you just kicked that man out of my house."

"Divina, it's none of your concern--"

"It absolutely is my concern. He was friends with Mom."

Marc stood behind Divina. He was deathly quiet. His mind had processed it quickly, understood it almost immediately. Claude. No way was that an interesting coincidence.

Marc gently placed his hands on Divina's shoulders. "What," she asked, turning her head to look at him, and then quickly returning her gaze to Belinda. He opened his mouth to answer, but when he couldn't come up with how to say it, he kept quiet. "He traveled a long way," Divina said.

Belinda took this in. "So, it was no accident he was here?"

"Really, Belinda! He's been here before. You don't get lost in places where you've traveled to before."

"When was he here," she asked suddenly, the worry running over her words.

"You remember. He was here at the funeral. We talked to him."

"Yes, but that was in town."

"He visited Mom, too, right before she passed away. Don't you remember that?"

"Yes, I remember," Belinda replied weakly.

"What did he do? Should I be afraid of him if he comes back? If Claude is here..." Her voice drifted off.

Belinda was glad she made the connection, so she wouldn't have to sit down and explain it to her. There was enough pain in assuming, but actually having to say everything out loud would be devastating.

"Claude?" Divina's voice was high, questioning. There was no doubt her mind was rapidly flipping through the scenarios.

"Divina, sit down, let me tell you--"

"You can tell me one thing. Tell me it's not true. Whatever I'm thinking," Divina said, the sentences sprinting from her mouth, one after the other without pausing. Before Belinda could reach Divina, the young woman was already out the door. She was obviously chasing after the intruder.

Marc gave Belinda a sympathetic look conveying his feelings on the situation. Divina didn't need this. He was gone in an instant, trailing after her. Especially now, he refused to leave her alone with the new face.

Belinda bent down, picking up the bigger pieces of the shattered dish on the floor. Her hands were shaking.

The trees were black shadows, blacker than even the night sky. They twisted and turned in turmoil, lining every view the eyes could see. The breeze was humming softly, thrashing the tops of the branches and swaying the grass on the ground. The birds had silenced their songs, and insects lowered their sounds to a ceaseless and unnoticeable blurry monotony of noise. The chill was evident beneath the cloudless uniform of the sky.

Divina wasn't sure the chill was nature or already inside her. She knew instantly which way he had gone, and she ran in that direction. No one gets away that easy. Not from this. Within a few moments, she could hear the lazy footsteps not far in front of her. Her instinct also told her she was being followed. She didn't want Marc to intrude, but she secretly appreciated his presence. Trying to place the reminder to thank Marc later, she put him in the back of her mind. "Wait," she yelled.

The footsteps ahead of her stopped. The dark figure turned around. He seemed taller in the dark. She ran up to him, went around him, and they stood face to face while she blocked his path.

"I really shouldn't be here," Claude said.

"Claude. That's not the most common name," she spat at him. There was such hurt in her eyes. Marc joined them, standing behind Claude.

"I feel kind of cornered," Claude said warily.

"There's a good explanation for that. You are cornered," Marc replied.

"You weren't my mother's friend, were you?" Her eyes were narrowed, her pose angry and in pain all at the same time. Her thoughts begged him to say she had misunderstood. What she was thinking contained all the things her mother had never been capable of doing.

Claude was quiet. He looked at Marc as if Marc may force him to answer. "Don't look at me like that," Marc said. "I'm just here for her. I'm staying out of this."

"Thanks," Divina said to Marc.

"I was Rebecca's friend," Claude finally said, choosing his words carefully. There was no lie in that.

Divina felt her spine in her back as surely as if it was pushing against the inside of her skin. The tiny hairs on the back of her neck stood straight up. It had been years since she had heard anyone other than family say her mother's name. The result was electric. Even her mere name on someone else's lips caused Divina to have a severe reaction. She rolled her eyes. "Fine, we'll play this your way. You were more than my mother's friend? That's a yes or no answer."

Claude held up a hand between them as if he could stop the question in the air. "Let me explain--"

"Yes or no," she said defiantly.

Claude pressed his lips together tightly. He merely shook his head slightly, so slightly that she had to be staring to catch it. The nod was in agreement.

Divina looked ready to sucker punch him. Marc wondered if he would have to protect the stranger from Divina and not vice versa.

"It's not what you're thinking," Claude said to her.

"Don't presume to tell me what I am thinking."

Claude's eyes softened. She was just like her mother, so independent. This girl wasn't going to take anything from anyone. A rush of pride swept over him from an unknown place. Rebecca had done what she had always wanted, raised her children, not even realizing she had left these pieces of her behind in them. "Your mother and I were together many years before she met your father."

Divina jerked her head. Obviously, he had her full attention.

"She was the one great love of my life," he continued.

The brittle frozen glare Divina had been using thawed. Maybe things were not as she thought. "Go on," Divina said.

"It's a long story," Claude said, his voice very tired. He wasn't sleepy, but the whole situation had taken so much out of him.

163

"I've got the time," Divina said. There was no way she was going to let him leave now. He knew her mother.

"How about tomorrow? I was planning on staying in a hotel down the road about two miles. There's a diner in there, right?"

"I'll meet you there for lunch at noon," Divina said.

"Okay," Claude replied, and he began to walk around her.

She put her hand on his shoulder as he passed, stopping him in his tracks. Divina stared straight into his eyes. Claude almost felt intimidated.

"Don't think about leaving," she said. "Because I will find you. I don't care how far you go."

A quick smile that didn't hold much joy played across his lips. "Determined. Just like your mother."

She was silent.

"I'll be there." With that, he was gone.

Marc walked close to where Divina stood. "Are you all right?" Divina stared until Claude was no longer visible. "Divina?"

"What?" She paused. "Oh, yeah. I'm fine."

"I'm not all that convinced," he said.

"Sorry," she said, lowering her gaze to the ground in front of her. "I can try again." She put a fake smile on her face. "I'm fine," she said too loudly and with a giddy voice that didn't belong to her.

"I don't know what to tell you."

"There isn't anything you can say, Marc. If there was, I'd tell you to say it."

"Just let me know if anything comes up," he said. "Get me up in the middle of the night. I'll say whatever you need to hear."

"Thanks. What did I do to deserve you?"

"Goes both ways," he said kindly.

They walked back to the farm. Belinda was in the kitchen. The shattered pieces of the dish still weren't cleaned up. Divina instinctively shot her aunt an angry look without thought.

"What happened," Belinda asked, more to Marc than Divina although they both stood side by side.

Divina didn't look as if she would have answered had she even been asked.

"We talked to him," Marc replied.

Divina spoke. "I'm meeting with him tomorrow."

"That's not a good idea--" Belinda began.

"Belinda," Divina said, a clear warning in her voice, "you don't get to decide what ideas are good anymore. Or what secrets to keep."

Walking with her head high, she briefly waved good night at Marc, and then she left the room with Belinda staring after her.

"She's upset," Marc said to Belinda.

"She has reason to be."

"You might want to tell me what's going on," he said.

"How much does she know?"

"Claude only said that he knew Rebecca years before she met Divina's father. He said that she was the great love of his life."

"That's it?"

"How much more is there?"

"You might want to sit down," Belinda said to Marc, offering him a chair. They sat there long into the night while Belinda told him the story. When it ended, Marc sat in silence. He didn't know what to say or how to act, if he should tell Divina right now or let Claude do it.

"Wow," he muttered under his breath.

"It's going to destroy her."

"No," Marc said to Belinda. The old woman looked as if she was about to cry.

"Trust me. Divina is stronger than that. She'll handle it. It may take a while, but she will understand."

"But she thinks her mother was an angel on earth, a saint. That's her mother we're talking about. The mother she barely knew and hardly remembers. The woman could do no wrong in Divina's eyes."

"Divina is smart. She knows her mother was human. Don't worry, Belinda. This could be much, much worse."

Belinda gave him a small, warm look. "Yes, you're right. It could be worse."

Marc patted her crossed hands on the table before he stood to go. "I'll take care of her," he said sincerely.

Belinda slowly raised her head, and her eyes came out from under their heavy lids. She didn't need to say anything. Marc could see the gratefulness written all over her face.

When he got out of the house, he felt the tension in his gut. Honestly, he didn't know how Divina was going to react. Of all the times when he had nothing comforting to say, this was going to be the worst. He knew that for a fact. What words were there?

Chapter 18

Divina stirred all night. Sleep only visited a few moments at a time. John didn't notice. He had no idea anything out of the ordinary had happened or was going to occur again at noon the next day.

She crawled out of bed early and stowed away behind the locked door of the bathroom. Divina stared at her face in the mirror. With a brush of her hair and a dusting of light powder, she was ready long before time to start out for the diner. Clothing was an obstacle. Most of her clothing that was good enough to wear out had belonged to her mother. Finally, she found a long yellow skirt and deep green tank top that John had given her a few Christmas's ago. She slipped her feet into matching green ballet slippers that served as dress shoes but were comfortable. When she wasn't in work boots, these were what she was in.

Deciding there were worse things in life than being early, Divina crept out of the house before Marc went to look in on her and see if she was awake. Part of him wanted to follow, but another part told him that if she had wanted him there, she would have let him know. He decided to let her be.

The diner wasn't crowded. A few women recognized Divina and embraced her in boring conversation, so by the time they left, it was noon. When she saw Claude come through the door, she felt a great sense of relief. For some reason, she hadn't believed he would run off, but she also didn't trust herself enough to be sure. Even as a child, she had instantly trusted him. She remembered.

"Good morning," he said as he took a seat.

She smiled in acknowledgment. "Did you sleep well?" Her face showed she was still skeptical of him, but she was trying.

"Actually, no," he answered. "I tossed and turned all night. Believe it or not, you have me quite nervous."

Divina relaxed. "What," she asked him when she noticed how he was looking so curiously at her.

"Sorry," he said, placing his napkin in his lap. "You just remind me of her. Not just in how you look, but the way your face moved, your gestures and expressions. It's all very strange. Good, don't get me wrong, but strange."

"I'm sure it is, but be aware that I am not like my mother in many, many ways. I doubt I'm anything like her. I didn't even know her."

"That's truly a sad thing. She was brilliant."

Divina liked how he talked of her. She felt he loved her by the way his voice melted when he spoke of her. This man may say things that will change her view of her mother, but as of right now, she welcomed him and his words of her.

Claude began the story of Rebecca, of how they met, and of their love.

"Wow," Divina said, entranced. It was like a fairy tale.

Then, he went on to how Rebecca wanted children and family, wanted dreams that he couldn't give her. It didn't mean they cared for each other any less.

Divina had been waiting for the fight that would have made her mother leave him, been waiting for the other woman, but there was none. Her mother knew her life was destined for different things, for Divina's life.

He told her about the pictures she sent him.

"We never really let go," he said to Divina. "I certainly couldn't."

"Did you ever meet anyone else? Get married? Do you have children?"

Claude smiled at her interest. "No, I don't have kids, never got married. I'm a painter. My life is structured around me being solitary."

"Then, how did my mother come into the scene?"

"She came in and fit perfectly. It was like I had my own little world, and one day, this amazing woman came in and decided she wanted to live there with me. So, she stayed for a long time."

"Was it hard?"

"The transition was smooth. Once she was there, I didn't know how I ever lived happily without her. When she left, I saw how lonely the loft was without her presence."

"The loft?"

"We lived in my loft in New York. It's basically a big room full of all my paintings, and it's where I do all my work."

"Was she the only woman who ever lived there with you?" Divina was a child again, asking all the questions without hesitation, without scanning her thoughts first.

168

"No, I had many women come in and out because I painted them. They weren't girlfriends or even lovers. There was no woman who was home to me after Rebecca. No one else visited my little world, and certainly, no one lived there with me."

"So, you really loved her?"

"Love her. Until the day I die."

"It's like you were married, but without the ceremony."

"Basically, although she may not have said that. The first man she was completely committed to for her life was your father."

"So, why is Belinda so upset about this?"

Claude hesitated.

Divina wasn't about to let him stop now. There was more to the story, and he knew she knew it.

"Belinda may not have all the facts," he said.

"Well then, you tell me the facts."

"When your grandfather died--"

"My mother's father?"

"Yes, when he died, Rebecca had to come back to New York."

"Why?"

"She had some of his things in the loft. They were left there when she left me."

"You couldn't just send them?"

Claude laughed and ran his fingers through his hair. "We could have, but I think she wanted to see me."

"This isn't going to be the only time you see her again, is it?" Divina felt the betrayal in her bones.

"She needed someone who knew her like I did, especially when she got sick."

"That's how you knew to come to the house."

"Yes--"

"Was that the only time you came to the house?"

"Yes, and this past week. Those were the only times. Rebecca always traveled to see me in New York. But it wasn't what you're thinking--"

"Did she stay with you?"

"Yes." Claude knew from the look on her face that the answer he gave wasn't the one she wanted.

"So, she had an affair."

"No!"

Divina was startled by the rise in his voice.

"It wasn't like that. We just talked."

Divina scoffed. She didn't buy it; it sounded too much like a line.

"Seriously. We were friends. She wasn't cheating on your father for all those years."

"Did she still love you?"

"I believe she did. What we had doesn't vanish when you meet someone else."

"So, are you saying nothing ever happened? You never kissed her? She never held you a little too long? It was completely innocent?" Divina wanted to force him to admit to it, to admit to something.

"Do you remember when she got better? I guess it was right before she got pregnant."

"Yes," Divina said, then the memory hit her out of nowhere. "All the trips she took." Her voice was soft. Claude said nothing. "All those times she went away. They were all to see you."

"Yes, they were."

Divina sat with this for a moment before she was ready to continue. "Okay. So, what happened during the time she was better?"

"She only visited me once during that time. It was the last time she came to New York, but I didn't know it was going to be the last--"

"Shortly after, she was pregnant?" Divina's mind began to jump.

"That's what must have happened because she died less than a year later."

"You're Claude's father?"

"God, no," he said, shocked.

"No?" She didn't bother to hide the happiness in her voice.

"Rebecca never would have done that to you or your father. She didn't have it in her, but..."

"But what?"

"There was a kiss," he said with guilt.

"That's it," she said, the relief filtering through.

"It wasn't all that innocent," he said, remembering.

"I don't care. So, you kissed her. But that was it?"

"You're not upset?"

"No," she said incredulously.

170

"I would have kept her in the loft for the rest of her life if she would have let me," he said sadly. "I know that's a terrible thing to say because of you and your brother and your father, but I would have kept her there. I would have taken her back."

Divina reached over and placed her hand on his arm. "It's okay. You can stop feeling bad now."

"I can't believe I'm talking to you."

"I can't understand why Belinda is so upset about this."

"I can. I'm sure Rebecca never told her details about that night. She probably thinks I am the father. Your mother never dreamed your father would follow in her footsteps so quickly. She thought she was leaving you kids in his care. I'm sure she didn't want Belinda telling him anything to make him doubt their love. Just the fact that the child is named after me is enough to cause him to question her loyalty."

"And you're sure that you're not the father?"

"Divina," he said with great sincerity, "it's physically impossible."

She smiled. "Then, that's the end of that."

"I honestly didn't know you were here. I thought the house was empty."

"Why did you want to buy it?"

"It's simple, really. My work is finally doing well. And of course, I am still holding onto a memory. Mostly, I wanted to see the place, see if I could still feel her there."

"She really loved that house in the beginning, before it started to fall apart."

"She loved it even when it fell apart. I'm sure of that. She never did have roots before that place."

"Were you planning on living there?"

"I don't know for sure," he said, even his voice conveying his lack of decision.

"Sorry, but it's not for sale."

"I know. It was good to see it, though. I could never have stayed there anyway. She is still there. It would drive me mad."

"Yeah, I guess she is."

"I should probably be going. I have to get back home," he said. "Lunch is on me."

Divina was surprised. It felt like he had just got here. Did she have to lose this link to her past already?

He saw her face and said, "We can keep in touch, if you want. I would stay longer, but I really can't."

"All right. We'll keep in touch?"

"Here," Claude said, handing her a platinum white business card. "Rebecca would have a fit if she saw I had my own business card."

"Thanks. I'll use this."

"I'm looking forward to it," he said as he got up.

They shook hands, kindly but firmly. There was still a lot of ground to cover to reach a place where they would be completely comfortable with one another. Claude knew before he turned to wave from the door that she would be watching him walk away. He smiled at her standing, staring after his exit. Rebecca used to do that to him all the time. He could almost feel her presence watching him, wondering what he thought. In his mind, he told her that Divina was perhaps the loveliest daughter he had ever seen. She had done well. He was so proud of his love.

* * * * *

Divina burst into Belinda's small bedroom.

"How'd it go," Belinda asked carefully.

"It's not what you think," Divina said to her strongly.

Belinda raised her eyebrows as she thought Divina had been had. The man had said magic words and made her believe him.

"She didn't cheat on Dad."

"Claude said that?"

"They were in love, but it never went that far. That's what he said."

"And you believe him," Belinda asked seriously, putting a lot of stake in Divina's opinion.

"I believe him."

"That's great, honey. Maybe it is the truth--"

"I know there were trips, many trips. She went to New York to see him. On that last trip out there, I think her life almost changed, but she didn't do it. She couldn't do it to us."

Belinda wrapped her arms around Divina. "Of course, she couldn't. She wouldn't hurt you for the world."

"I was so scared," Divina said, holding Belinda tightly. "I didn't want Claude to not be my..."

172

"Claude will always be your brother. No matter what."

"I know, but it still frightened me."

"Of course it did. It would be a shock to anyone."

Divina kissed Belinda on the cheek before leaving the room. All Belinda could do was pray to God that what Claude had said was true. Rebecca had never gone into detail. She said that she didn't want her sister to be disappointed in her. Rebecca said that she couldn't hurt her family, but she had done one last thing before she left Claude for good, permanently.

Belinda had never been so happy about a kiss.

* * * * *

"How are you," Marc asked as Divina joined him in a building filled with grain. His words were careful. He was testing the waters.

Before she knew what she was doing, Divina threw her arms around Marc's neck. "It's not what you think," she said. "What Belinda told you never happened. She misunderstood. They were in love, and she stole away to see him during her marriage, but she didn't cheat on my father!"

"That's great," he said, lightly letting his arms rest around her.

Divina backed away just enough to look at his face.

"Thanks for not following me," she said.

"If you had wanted me there, you would have asked. I am glad everything worked out."

"Were you worried?"

"No, of course not," he said, although it was obvious he had been.

She leaned his head on his shoulder. "I'm glad. It's nice to be worried about sometimes."

"Then, you should feel nice a lot."

She smiled. That's when Marc inhaled the scent of her shampoo, and he couldn't control it this time. More than anything, he wanted to kiss her. Instead, he backed up at lightening speed. "Are you okay," she asked him quickly, her mouth confused and turning down at the corners.

"I just remembered, I have something really important to do," he said, and then he was gone in an instant.

She looked outside of the building to see which way he went, but he was gone so quickly. He was out of sight before she could mutter another word. Divina cursed at herself for making him uncomfortable.

173

By the time Marc has slipped into a nearby building, his heart was racing. This was just plain wrong. Divina was Edgar's sister, and most importantly, his boss's wife. Whatever he thought that was, he was wrong. He decided to convince himself that nothing happened. He really did have to do something. If only he could figure out what that was.

Chapter 19

John heard the whole story second hand from Belinda. He hadn't even known Claude had come into his house. He felt like such an outsider. Divina could see the hurt he felt from being left out when he asked her about the meeting with Claude.

"I was going to tell you," she said, "the next time we had a conversation."

"We never have conversations. You're too busy running away from me," John retorted.

"Well, you're too busy at work to make the time," she snapped back.

"If I could be at home taking care of some children, then work wouldn't be getting in the way."

"Fine. I'll give birth and you stay home. In fact, I don't even need to give birth. You've got the money. Go buy a baby."

"That's not what I meant."

"Yeah, I know what you meant. If I had kids and was staying at home, then you would make time for me."

"Now, you're putting words in my mouth."

"You're using imaginary children as the easy road to happiness."

"Think about it, though. They would change everything."

"This is getting us nowhere. I'm not bringing my children into a situation which is already full of chaos."

"You think our marriage is chaos?"

"You don't?"

"What did you mean by *your* children? I would have to be involved, you know."

"This isn't working," Divina said, exasperated. "Is this really us trying to work things out?"

"Yes," he shouted.

She looked up above as if she expected God to come down and take her side.

"My head hurts," John said, rubbing his temples.

She didn't smile. Her eyes felt void of emotion.

"What's that look about," he asked her.

"What look?"

"That one on your face right now."

"I'm not making a look."

"Do you want me to go get a mirror?"

"Never mind. I didn't realize I was making a *look*. God forbid my face forms an expression."

"You know what I meant. You look like this is all worth nothing to you, like talking to me means nothing."

"It doesn't mean nothing. It accomplishes nothing."

"Do you honestly think things were better when we barely spoke?"

"We don't speak now. This is not speaking, John. This is bickering."

"No, it's communication."

She put her head in her hands and covered her face for a few seconds.

"Good, Divina. If you can't see me, then I'm not here."

"Shut up," she snapped.

"Come on, look at me."

She put her hands down and looked at him, obviously annoyed.

"Now, let's talk like we're rational adults. Rational, married adults."

"Okay," she said, crossing her arms, eager to see if this may lead to a good place, to a different place than where they were right now.

The phone in his pocket rang. She sarcastically smiled and shook her head as if she had known this was coming.

"This will only take me a minute."

She pretended to check her watch and time his minute.

He got off the phone in three minutes, which was a record in itself.

"Where were we," he asked, his mind coming back from the business track.

"I give up," she said to no one in particular.

"Great. Walk away. You've been treating this marriage like a joke the whole time anyway."

"Where did that come from?"

"You know it's true. If you cared about your marriage, you'd--"

"I'd what? Have kids? Buy a bonnet? I don't see how you can say that to me, Mr. I Work All the Time and Want Complete Control Over

176

Everything."

"You're the one who doesn't tell me about strangers who come by and who bring on all these conversations."

"If I didn't bring up these conversations, we'd never talk at all."

"No, we'd talk, but it would be about--"

"The weather? Business?"

"Isn't that better than screaming all the time?"

"For who? Basically, you want me to nod."

He let out a deep sigh.

"I took my vows seriously. We went before God and everyone. When I married you, it was because I believed in what we were doing. It was for the long haul."

"Sure, for five whole minutes of your life."

"If that was true, I would have left you a long time ago."

"You couldn't."

"Why not?"

"Because I wouldn't let you. Unlike you, I married you for the rest of my life. I'm going to keep fighting until it starts working."

"Even if that means we are fighting for the rest of our lives? You'll be miserable. You can't say you won't be."

"Yeah, well, I won't be divorced."

"You're the one who keeps bringing up ending the marriage. We have some problems, so you make some threats and grand proclamations on how wonderful you are and how terrible I am."

"That's not true--"

"Oh, sorry. I'm just the one who got married to try it out. If it didn't work, why should I care," she said sarcastically.

"If the glass slipper fits--"

"I really wouldn't compare this to a fairy tale if I was you."

"You can be so stubborn sometimes."

"I can?" Divina was incredulous.

"That's what I said."

"John, I'm tired. I have to finish up work."

"I figured it was about the time you were going to leave. Happens every time. No wonder we don't make progress."

"Yeah, because we all know if I stayed here, things would magically come together. We'd go skipping hand in hand across the lawn in fifteen minutes. This is a dead end street, and I am not having the same fight with you right now."

"Fine. Go."

She turned and went.

"We'll finish this when you get done," he shouted after her.

Divina had a mind to just stay out and sleep in the barn with the cows. Telling herself to be an adult, she went to see John after she got done. He barely said a word to her. For tonight, the fight was over.

A few nights later, she was working and venting to Marc, who had seemed to return to their relationship as if nothing odd had happened. "I just don't know anymore," she said. "I forget what I am doing in this. Does that make sense?"

"It makes a lot of sense. I don't want to interfere, but, Divina, you're not happy. I see it. You're living every day in complete peril and conflict."

"I can't just up and leave him."

"Oh, no, I didn't mean that," Marc said, catching himself. In his head, he asked himself what kind of person he was becoming, practically telling her to end her marriage. "You just have to find a way to fight but also find some peace within it, you know?"

"Thanks," she said. "I'm not unhappy all the time. I'm happy when I'm with you." She scooted by him to enter another room, and as she past, she patted his cheek with one of her hands. "Too bad I didn't know you before. I would have married you instead."

"Shit," Marc said under his breath as she slid out of the room. She was joking with her friend, but he was glad she hadn't heard him, hadn't seen his face. He told himself that this had to be a phase. He had to tell himself that. He couldn't live like this for much longer. He was listening to her talk about her husband for goodness sake.

The weeks went on, and some of the work became lighter. Divina and John were still having problems although things were coming to a more peaceful place. They were fighting less but avoiding each other more. Marc didn't tell her that he couldn't take it anymore, watching them fight, listening to her speak. He absolutely wasn't going to tell her why. He felt like a silly schoolboy. He definitely didn't tell her when he handed John his resignation.

* * * * *

"Do you just want me to pick someone for you, or do you want to do it," John asked Divina as she was brushing her teeth that night.

"What are you talking about?"

"You know, to take Marc's place. He'll be gone within the week. I figured you'd probably want to do it, but if you don't, I will."

Divina kept brushing her teeth as if nothing happened. He didn't see the muscles in her arms tense up and her eyes open wide as saucers.

"I'll do it then, okay?" He left the doorway as she nodded in agreement.

She spat out the toothpaste and walked fast out into the hall. "I forgot something," she yelled to him. "I'll be right back in." Grabbing her coat from the hook by the door, she disappeared outside.

Marc lived in a little house down the side of the premises. Many employees lived on the land. He was quiet and considerate. Divina had barely been in his home. She didn't care what time it was when she started pounding on his door.

"Marc," she yelled as she noticed lights being turned on with each room closer to the front door.

He flung the door open. "What's wrong? What happened?" His hair was disheveled. It was obvious he had been resting if not sleeping.

Divina didn't care. "What the hell do you mean you're leaving? It's a joke, right? Because I know you'd tell me if you were leaving."

"It's true," he sad quietly. "I got another job."

"Where," she asked, looking as if she wanted to cry and throw something at the same time.

"The Midwest. It's a good job."

She stood speechless.

"You know I was going to tell you."

"When? In a letter? An hour before you packed up and walked away? You're supposed to be my best friend! Why?"

"It's--"

"Just ask, and we'll do it. We'll match their offer. Do you want better hours?"

"It's nothing like that."

"Then what? Marc, why would you leave?"

"Because--"

"You have family here," she said honestly, referring to herself and Edgar. Although most of the lights inside the house were on and filtered softly through the closed curtains, Marc hadn't switched on the outside light. Their faces were masked in shadows. She was wearing a heavy brown jacket and a white cotton nightgown, which fell below her knees. Marc was wearing a tee shirt and some really old striped pajama pants. His feet were bare, and her hair was short but thick and whipping in the night wind. His face had such defined lines and sunken cheekbones that the shadows attached to him without mercy.

Divina realized how beautiful his face was and how deep his kind, dark brown eyes were. She wasn't prepared for what he did next.

Marc took on step out, and without putting a hand on her, kissed her.

At that moment, all other thoughts were erased, and nothing else existed. She didn't know when or how her arms went around his shoulders or when his hands touched her hair or her lower back. His lips were warm and soft, and they tilted their heads as if they had been doing this together for years. Their eyes were closed gently, daring to open but never wanting to look for fear that this wasn't really happening. It was deep and raw and consuming.

In all her years of marriage, John had never kissed her like that.

When she realized what was happening and regained the ability to move away from the dreamy phase she was in, she took two large leaps backwards. The tips of her fingers went to her lips, and she stared at him. The shock was evident.

Marc didn't say a word.

Her eyebrows lowered over her eyes almost in sadness. She just gestured towards the house she shared with John. He understood. She walked away, trying to walk without falling, without tripping. She faltered once, and Marc stood still on his doorway. His instinct was to step out and go to her, help her up, make sure she was all right, but she didn't even turn around when she made another motion for him to stay where he was. She kept walking, and within a few moments, she was back in her house.

Marc stayed in the doorway. He couldn't stop staring even if now what he was staring at was only where she had just been.

Divina crawled into bed with John as if nothing had happened. No words were said. John was already close to sleep anyway. She saw no need to bring it up. She squinted her eyes shut and waited for sleep.

When morning came, John woke up to find a note.

Dear John,

Had to make a trip on business. Took flight his morning. I'll be

home before tomorrow morning. Don't worry about me. You
know I wouldn't just up and leave unless it was important.
Love,
Divina

John shook his head at the note as if Divina was there to see his reaction. He didn't give it a second thought.

Divina took the first flight going out in the morning. The directions were perfect, and as she stood at his door, she felt an odd tingle run through her. Claude opened the door and smiled. Her mother had stood in that exact spot.

"You look terrible," he remarked. "Come on in."

Divina came in. The place looked exactly as he had described on the phone. The two had kept in close touch. She told him he was like the uncle she never had or even really wanted. Claude told her stories and wanted to learn all about Divina's life. She was a lot like her mother, and he liked seeing Rebecca living on. Claude also knew that with Mr. Hamilton gone, Rebecca would have appreciated it if he made sure to keep an eye on her. Although Claude barely knew the girl, he would have done anything already to keep her safe. Rebecca loved Divina, so therefore, Claude had an attachment to her, too.

She walked in and saw the absence of furniture.

"That's the same thing your mother thought," he said at her reaction. "She always tried to get me to go furniture shopping."

"I can hear her," Divina said. Then, she made her voice go a little higher as she remembered her mother's voice and said, "Just let me buy one chair. One."

Claude laughed. "Exactly. But you didn't come here to discuss my decorating. Something must have really troubled you."

Divina tucked her hair behind her ears in nervousness. She looked about ready to start running around the apartment, like she was a caged animal wanting to be free. "I'm a terrible person," she said, almost sobbing.

Claude looked at her sharply. "No, you're not. Good people sometimes make mistakes. What have you done that is so terrible?"

"I'm just like my mother," she hissed, her face scrunched up, the words showing that this was not a favorable way to be.

"I hope so."

"No, you don't understand. My best friend kissed me."

"Oh."

181

"I'm married. I don't run around and cheat on my husband." She put her head in her hands.

"That doesn't mean anything, then--"

"No, you still don't get it. I don't even understand it."

Claude paused a moment. Then, he came up with the right questions. "It was a good kiss then?" Her look said that he already knew the answer to that. "You really have a thing for this guy?'

"A thing," she asked with amazement, as if she wished it could as simple as just a thing.

"You're in love with him," Claude stated with surprise.

"I didn't say that!" Her words flowed very quickly, defensively. He waited. No denial was forthcoming. She merely made a whimper.

Claude knew all about her marriage. She had told him many things about her past. He knew she wasn't in love with her husband when she married him. He knew she may have fallen in love with him, even for a moment, but he wasn't sure, even if there had never been someone else in the equation, that the marriage would last.

"Marriage isn't something I take lightly!" She spoke as if this was going to surprise him, too.

"I know. Of course not, otherwise you wouldn't have been married for so long."

"John and I have our problems, but I didn't go off searching to find someone else. I never would do that. Who doesn't have problems?"

"But, Divina, most couples have good times, too."

"We've had good times! Well, I mean, we figured we would someday."

"This guy really got to you, didn't he?"

"He's been my best friend, the one person who knows me, and he's been there for more years than I can count," she said, saying the words but not listening to them.

Claude was careful not to give her advice. This had to do with her happiness, not his. He wasn't going to tell her to go for the underdog just because somehow he had been the underdog with Rebecca.

"But he's leaving--"

"John?"

"No, Marc. He quit his job."

Claude nodded and said before he thought, "He probably can't watch you with your husband anymore. You said he's your best friend, so I suppose you talked to him a lot about John."

"Oh, no," she said, realizing what she must have been putting Marc through all this time.

"Sorry, I didn't mean to make you think of that."

"It's okay," she said, putting a hand up. "I don't know how I am going to be there without him. He's the one source of happiness in my day. If he weren't there, I would never laugh. I wouldn't."

"When was the last time John made you laugh?"

She thought hard for a moment. "I don't remember."

"Divina, I can't tell you what to do or how to make this all go away."

"I know," she said. "I think I just needed to talk to someone out loud about it. I need to hear myself think. I'm so confused. It's like he just punched me, and I don't know anything anymore."

"I will tell you some things. You can't live your life unhappy, waiting for good things to happen or for people to change. You aren't going to be able to make Marc not care about you. You aren't going to be able to leave a marriage without guilt. This is your life, Divina. You, of all people, understand that what you have inside of you is a precious thing."

"Thank you, Claude."

"You are getting to spend your life with someone. Many people go through life and never fall in love, not once. I fell in love once, and it was worth everything, but I didn't get to share my life with her. I didn't grow old with her. You have someone who wants to grow old with you."

"I know."

"You have to decide what you want. You have to pick your life. I know you're young, and I know that you think you've already made all your decisions. You were barely twenty when you married John. I know you married him for good. But things change and things happen, and if you want your life to be different, then you have the power now."

"I don't know what I want."

"Just know, I will be here no matter what you do. I will always be a plane ride away or a phone call." Divina let a tear slip from her eye. She realized no one had ever said that to her before. "I'm proud of you," Claude said.

That's when Divina really started crying.

* * * * *

183

"You did what," Edgar asked Marc, stunned.

"I really don't want to repeat it all over again."

"I can't believe you kissed my sister."

"Don't forget, I quit my job, too."

"Wow, man, you're having a hell of a week."

Marc smiled. He was relieved that Edgar was so laid back. He took the news easily.

"I knew you'd leave someday. You know, I'm going to miss you and everything, but you're not exactly working in a lifetime career here."

"It was good, though, right? While it lasted?"

Edgar reached out and shook his friend's hand. "Yeah, it was the best."

"I haven't seen her today. I'm pretty much terrified."

"You didn't hear," Edgar asked. Marc was cautious as he gave Edgar a look that said that he hadn't heard anything. "Divina got on a plane this morning. No one really knows what she's doing. Supposedly business related. You must have really messed with her head."

Marc closed his eyes and tilted his head towards the sky, letting out a large breath. "For once, I know what I'm doing. But it doesn't matter, because what I am doing isn't helping anyone."

"Relax. You never know. If I got to pick, she'd dump John and shack up with you. You both could live in your little house a fifth of a mile from John."

"That's so not funny."

"I'm just trying to make you laugh. I'm just saying, don't dismiss my sister yet. She's got a lot more to her than everyone thinks."

"Thanks. You're a good guy."

Edgar smiled at the compliment. He knew that nice words only meant as much as who they were coming from, and Marc was the highest person on his list.

Chapter 20

Divina flew back on the latest flight. When she got in, John was asleep. She had been trying to figure everything out on the plane. No plane ride was long enough to determine what to do with a lifetime. Then, she did something she had never done before.

With a very large shove and an even louder voice, she said, "Wake up, John."

"Go to sleep."

"John, I need to talk to you."

"It can wait until tomorrow."

Divina turned on every light in the room.

"Fine, just hurry up, so I can back to sleep."

"This is serious."

"I'm up. I swear."

"I've been thinking all night--" she began.

"Can you just get to the point where this includes me?" He didn't realize it then, but he had just made the worst move of his life.

Divina looked at her husband, at this man she had vowed to love forever, and knew inside that she felt about as big and important as a bug on a windshield. "I'm sorry," she said.

"Okay," he said, and then he proceeded to curl up like he was going back to sleep.

Her next words woke him right back up.

"I'm leaving you."

He sat straight up. "What?"

"I don't want to be married anymore. I'm sorry. I know you'll be angry at first--"

"What the hell are you talking about? There is no way I'm giving you a divorce. Have you been drinking? Sleep it off. We'll talk about whatever problem is bothering you this week in the morning."

"I'm not in love with you."

"We're working on that, remember?"

"I'm a human being, John. You are, too. There is someone out there who you are going to fall in love with--"

"I'm already in love--"

"And she'll love you back. You don't love me. What we have isn't love. It's close, but it's something else."

"How would you know?" He asked her with great need. "You've never been in love. You're in love, but you just don't know it. Unless--"

"John, that's not--"

"You're in love with someone else!" John was on her feet now, pacing around her like a predator stalking its prey. He grabbed a vase off the dresser and held it in his hands.

"John, I would leave anyway. This isn't good for either of us--"

"Speak for yourself," he bellowed and threw the vase to the floor. The sound reminded her of thunder.

"Don't--"

"Who is it, huh? Just give me a name."

"It's no one. It has nothing to do with anyone but you and me--"

"Is that who you went to see? On the plane? Your other man?"

Divina opened her mouth and shut it again. She was glad he hadn't run out the door intent on killing Marc.

"I'm just going to call you in a couple days when you've calmed down," she said.

"You aren't leaving this house."

"There's another thing. I'm giving the old place to Edgar. He's going to move into the old house and tend to the fields there."

"No way. You can't give him things that are mine."

Divina's eyes narrowed with the urge to protect. "That house is in my name, left to me, and it remains mine. No part of it is yours. If you want me to give back the money it cost to restore it, then you can pay me for all the work I've been doing on this farm since we finished the house." John's jaw dropped. "It's Edgar's. You don't get to decide."

"What if he wants to stay and work here," John shot back.

"John, he hates it here. Even you can see that."

"I'm not going to make this easy on you."

"I know, John, but I don't want anything from you. Maybe someday, you'll be able to forgive me for this--"

"When you come back to me--"

"I'm not coming back, John. I'm sorry." Divina didn't take anything with her as she walked out of the house.

* * * * *

"Open the door," she yelled through Edgar's open window.

"Hey, Divina. How's it going," he asked cautiously.

She knew from the look on his face that he was pretty much up to speed. "I'm leaving John--"

"For Marc?"

"No, for me."

Edgar nodded in respect.

"I'm giving you the old house and land. I know you've been wanting it for a while. It's yours. I love you, Kid."

"Really? Divina, you don't have to--"

"Just give me a hug and let me get out of here before John comes after me. I need to leave for a few days and let him cool off. My life isn't here, and it's not in the old house either. John has no ties to our lands. Don't worry about him."

"He's upset?" Edgar already knew the answer to that.

"I'll call you," she said as she rustled his hair.

Edgar grabbed her and embraced her tightly. "I love you."

* * * * *

Marc's front door was open. Boxes were everywhere. He didn't see or hear her come in. When he saw a shadow coming across the carpet, he turned and saw her. "Oh, hi. Look, I'm really sorry about--"

He didn't get a chance to say another word because she kissed him quickly and in one sweeping gesture. Her stomach was churning, and she felt almost ill with the dizziness. Her whole body could feel it. Marc returned her kiss without reservation. They finally broke apart, but she didn't jump away this time.

"Wow," he remarked.

She stared deeply at him.

"Does this mean I get to help you be an adulterer," he asked without

187

humor. He didn't want to hear her say yes, but he certainly didn't want her to say no.

"I left John today, but I didn't do it for you."

"Okay," he said, not knowing what to assume.

"I did it for me. I had never been in love until I met you. And I don't know if you're in love with me or like me or just want me, but it doesn't matter."

"It doesn't matter? I don't believe that."

"It doesn't matter because I fell in love, and now that I've had that, I can't go back. I'm not happy here without you, so I am going to leave."

"When?"

"Right now."

"Can I come?"

Her face, close to his, broke into another one of her big smiles. "You want to come?"

"I'll go anywhere with you."

"I want to travel," she said. "I want to do all the things I've been saving for someday."

"Let's go," he said, grabbing her hands and kissing them.

"So, you're game for it?"

"Haven't you figured it out yet?"

"I'm not asking you to say you'll stay forever. I just know in my heart that this is worth it, even if it doesn't work. This moment right now," she said nodding her head, "was worth everything all on its own."

Marc kissed her lips, and just as the kiss ended, even before their eyes opened, he said what she already knew. "I love you."

"Let's get out of this place."

Hand in hand, leaving the majority of their belongings, Marc and Divina started down the path into town. Edgar saw them leave, his face smiling brightly in the dark. It couldn't have gone better if he had planned it himself.

Chapter 21

As for the rest of her life, Divina wasn't sure what would happen. She called and told Claude that night on the phone. When he hung up, he clapped his hands together in victory.

It was about time someone was happy.

Edgar took over the farm. It took a few years to prosper, but it was worth it. He even dabbled in a little furniture making. He worked hard and even married in his late twenties. He had three beautiful boys. He told them stories of their grandparents and their aunt, the wild one who ran off to see the world and comes back for holidays.

Belinda found out what happened from Edgar. She blamed Claude's influence, but knew there was nothing she could do. During a phone conversation with Divina, she said something that stuck out in Divina's mind. Mary had mentioned this would happen.

Divina was in love, Mary had told her, and the man was so kind and gentle. They would be very happy. When Belinda said she had known John was amazing for years, Mary had corrected her. John wasn't the one she had been talking about. Belinda moved into town and spent the rest of her life in the community among friends and keeping busy, finding joy in the every day.

Claude grew up fast and lived near Edgar and the old house. He had no recollection of his parents, so he treasured his siblings. The boy had a lot of support. He went on to school and became a businessman, helping Edgar with the paper work of the farm. Claude never was touched with the illness that they had been watching for during his life.

John didn't agree to the divorce at first. In fact, he fought it as hard as he could. After a few months of struggling, Edgar came over and said his piece. There was no yelling. Edgar made a lot of good points. John said that he couldn't let her go because he loved her, and Edgar told him that if that was true, then that would be the only reason he could let her go. Not long after that, John gave in. He stayed a workaholic, and he never remarried. He did, however, have two children with a kind woman who lived in one of the

189

nearby towns. His life may not have been as he had planned, but it had more joy than he had imagined.

Divina, well, she never regretted being married to John. She had been taught to never regret in a life but only to learn from the mistakes. Marc and Divina traveled all over the globe for the first six months.

They had the kind of love that people write songs about.

Eventually, they settled down in a suburb, and Marc went back to school. Claude was nearby when he was in his first few years of school. They were ironing out the rest of their lives. They went back to the old house often, especially when Edgar had children. They hadn't come to that place yet where they had decided one way or another. It was beginning to lean to one side though, because Divina thought that a little person made from the both of them may be the greatest miracle of her life so far.

She wasn't counting on forever, maybe not even tomorrow. It was during the times they went to all night movie marathons at a nearby cinema, and when they took walks in the fields a few miles out of the suburbs while the fire flies came alive, that she knew in her heart she had done the right thing. She had so many moments of peace. They fought, and times weren't always rosy, but when it came down to it, he was her match and she was his.

Marc and Divina never married, but their friend, Claude, knew. He winked at them whenever they parted from a visit like they were all sharing a secret.

Until death do us part. And, chances are, the love will live on after that, and life will still be good, because that love will be kept inside long after the end. Magic like that lives on, even if only in stories, in paintings. Somewhere out there, in a mess of colors that may be overlooked, is a red woman who is the definition of someone's life, someone's love.

The End

Printed in the United States
22321LVS00005B/439

9 781588 516510